AMISH INN MYSTERIES™

Homespun Homicide

Elizabeth Penney

Annie's®
AnniesFiction.com

Library of Congress-in-Publication Data
Homespun Homicide/ by Elizabeth Penney
p. cm.
I. Title
                    2017932766

AnniesFiction.com
(800) 282-6643
Amish Inn Mysteries™
Series Creator: Shari Lohner
Series Editor: Jane Haertel
Cover Illustrator: Kelley McMorris

10 11 12 13 14 | Printed in China | 9 8 7 6 5 4 3 2 1

1

Liz Eckardt typed the last number into the computer, then held her breath as she created the month-end report. She even closed her eyes for a moment and prayed.

She peeked, squinting at the bottom line. *Yes!* The inn's profits were up—again. After Liz closed her Boston law practice to purchase the Olde Mansion Inn in Pleasant Creek, Indiana, her decision had sometimes seemed like a foolish gamble. But her business was steadily growing, and, even better, she had reconnected with her mother's Amish relatives and made many new friends. The small, charming town was now her home.

The bulldog lying beside her desk gave a small woof as if reading her mind, something he seemed to do frequently. Beans had been an undisclosed part of the inn purchase, which disconcerted her at first. But he had soon won her heart, and now she couldn't imagine life without him.

Liz laughed. "And of course I'm happy to have you, Beans."

He groaned a reply before sinking back into slumber. Liz grinned and turned back to the computer. She hit the print button and the machine began to spit out a hard copy of the report.

"Knock, knock." Kiera Williams stood in the doorway of Liz's office. The thin, green-eyed young woman helped Liz keep the mansion grounds in order.

"Come on in." Liz pushed back her chair and stood, gathering the report and tucking it into a folder. "I'm ready for a break." She took a closer look at Kiera's face, which was smudged with dirt. "I can tell you've been out in the garden already."

Shifting from foot to foot, Kiera looked down at her grubby hands and soiled jeans. "I'm sorry. I should have washed up before coming in here." She cracked a huge grin. "But I couldn't wait to tell you. We have our first ripe tomato."

"Let's go look." Liz was almost as excited as her gardener about the prospect of fresh vegetables. Until this spring, she had focused on getting the extensive flower beds into tip-top shape. When Kiera had suggested putting in a vegetable garden, Liz had been leery about the upkeep. But the young woman kept everything meticulously weeded and watered.

Out in the garden, Kiera gave Liz a brief tour of the ripening vegetables—cucumbers, pole beans, peppers, and corn. Then she led the way to her pride and joy, the dozen tomato plants of different types and sizes.

"I was so excited this morning when I spotted this beauty." Kiera bent over to part the leaves. "I wanted you to be the first one to try it." She pointed to the vegetable. "Oh, no! Something ate it! It's *ruined*!"

Liz crossed a row of beets to join her, then bent to peer at the foliage. She saw tomatoes of all sizes and colors—big, small, green, and pink, and one large red one with a huge bite out of it. "That's a shame. It's gorgeous otherwise." Liz plucked the tomato and studied it, then tossed it toward the compost pile.

Kiera put her hands on her hips and glanced around, scowling. "I'd like to find the varmint that did that."

"You think a bird or animal chewed on it?" Liz turned to the bulldog, shuffling across the grass to join them. "It wasn't you, was it, Beans?" He just panted, tongue hanging out.

"Some dogs do like tomatoes. But he wasn't out here." Kiera plucked at her lip. "I sure hope the rest of the crop doesn't get eaten." She bent to study the ground. "I don't see any prints, but I'll keep my eyes open."

Before Liz could offer suggestions as to how to protect the garden, her part-time housekeeper, Sarah Borkholder, appeared at the inn's back door. Sarah was married to Isaac, the son of Liz's Amish cousin, Miriam.

"Liz, your guest has arrived," Sarah called.

"I'd better go," Liz said to her gardener. "We'll talk after I check in my guest."

"Okay." Crouching, Kiera began to pull weeds ferociously, "I just have a little more to do out here."

In the inn's foyer, a man wearing a polo shirt and crisp khakis waited near the check-in desk. Short with thinning dark hair, he had pouched eyes, hanging jowls, and a small but protuberant pot belly. Then Liz noticed the basset hound sitting at the man's feet.

She bit back an unfortunate laugh, tickled by the resemblance between the two. "Welcome to the Olde Mansion Inn." She held out her hand. "I'm Liz, the innkeeper."

He nodded as they shook hands. "I'm John Smith. I called this morning about two rooms."

Liz moved behind the desk. "Of course. Let me pull up your reservation." She tapped at the computer keys. "Will your traveling companion be arriving later?"

John gestured at the dog. "This is my companion. I need a room for him."

Being an innkeeper brought Liz into contact with many unusual people and situations. But this was a new one. "Are you saying you want to pay for a room for your dog?"

The man nodded, making his jowls quiver. "That's correct." He reached into his back pocket and pulled out a fat wallet. "I'll be happy to give you a deposit." He leafed through and pulled out a stack of bills. "I'll pay for four nights in advance."

This too was rare, being paid in cash, and Liz added a run to the bank to her to-do list. She also mentally rearranged the room assignments. Since the dog wouldn't need a bathroom—she thought—she could put them on the third floor, in the Sunrise and Sunset Rooms.

"That's very generous of you," Liz said. "If the dog doesn't make a mess, I'll happily return your deposit." She totaled the charges and gave him the figure.

John counted out large bills onto the counter. "He won't. He doesn't chew, scratch, or bark, and he's house-trained." He tucked away his now much-lighter wallet. "And I brought his bed with me."

Good. Liz had been wondering how to broach the topic. She really didn't want a dog sleeping on her linens. "I'm sure it won't be a problem. Many of my guests bring their pets."

Kiera and Beans entered the foyer, both reacting when they spotted the dog. Beans panted louder and picked up the pace slightly, while Kiera cried out and ran to the basset hound's side. "He's adorable." She bent to fondle his floppy ears. "What's his name?" She giggled. "Or is he a she?"

"He's a boy," John said dryly, busy signing the register. "His name is . . . ah, Rover."

Beans and the basset hound got acquainted while Liz finished the paperwork and Kiera watched. Liz grabbed the keys to the rooms. "I'll take you up."

John released the handle of his wheeled suitcase. "Come on . . . Rover."

The basset hound sighed and slumped to the floor, resting his head on his paws. Beans flopped beside him in an almost identical position.

"Isn't that cute? They're friends," Kiera said.

Liz paused at the foot of the staircase. "You can leave him here if you want. He's not bothering anyone."

"Come, Rover. Now." The dog didn't move. John hissed with

annoyance as he stamped a foot lightly. "I wanted to take him to his room."

"Do you have a leash?" Kiera asked. "I'll bring him up." She grinned. "I'm good with dogs."

John raised a brow as he eyed Kiera, his expression conveying disbelief that she could be any better with his pet than he was. But he bent to unclip a leash from the suitcase and gave it to her.

"We'll be in the Sunrise and Sunset Rooms, Kiera," Liz said.

Liz led the way to the third floor, moving slowly to accommodate her guest. At the top she opened the door to both rooms. "You can have your choice. The Sunset Room faces west, the Sunrise Room east, of course."

"Of course," John murmured. Setting his suitcase on the hall floor, he popped into both rooms, eyeing them closely. "I like what you've done."

Liz warmed at this unexpected praise. "Thanks. I wanted them simple but cheerful." Both rooms were furnished with a blend of contemporary and antique furniture, with white walls set off by colorful decorative touches.

John wheeled his suitcase into the Sunset Room. "Bright light bothers me in the morning so I'll take this one."

Liz placed both keys on the dresser. "I hope you enjoy your stay in Pleasant Creek." Then she thought of something. "Are you here for the Amish Arts and Crafts Fair?" The multicounty event held at the fairgrounds featured wonderful items ranging from candles to pieces of fine furniture.

He pulled his head back, thick brows drawing together in a scowl. "Amish Arts and Crafts? No, I'm here on personal business."

Liz's cheeks heated up at the implication she had been prying, but she merely said, "I heard it's going to be spectacular. One of my friends will be displaying furniture there. Jackson Cross, of Cross Furniture Company."

"Is that so?" John opened and shut a dresser drawer, appearing to admire how well it slid on its runners. Then he glanced around. "I suppose I'd better go get my dog. He needs his nap."

Liz heard panting and cajoling from the staircase. "If I'm not mistaken, he's on his way up."

They entered the hall to see a triumphant Kiera arriving at the top of the stairs, Rover trudging along behind her on his short legs. "Here he is. But I gotta tell you, he doesn't like his name. Either that or he's deaf. Never met a dog that didn't come when he was called."

John took the leash, murmuring thanks. "He's got his quirks, that's for sure. But don't we all?"

After Liz went back downstairs, she realized she felt uneasy leaving that much cash around. A walk to the bank was in order, and frankly, she would welcome a stroll in the summer sunshine. That was one thing she enjoyed about living in a small town as compared to Boston—the ability to make her rounds on foot.

On her way out of the inn, Liz stopped by Sew Welcome, the quilting store located in the front of the inn building. Owners Mary Ann Berne and Sadie Schwarzentruber bustled about, packing fabrics and notions.

Liz gazed around in bemusement. "Did I miss something?"

Mary Ann tossed her gray bob with a laugh. "We're not moving out, Liz. But we are closing the store for a few days."

"We decided to take a booth at the craft fair," Sadie said. "You're not required to be Amish to participate." Tall and strong despite being in her seventies, Sadie picked up and moved a full box with only a tiny grunt.

"That's right," Liz said. "Jackson is displaying his furniture.

But he does hire Amish workers, and his designs are based on the Amish style."

"They want traditional crafts—that's the only requirement." Mary Ann folded a handmade quilt. "From what I understand, we can sell directly to customers as well as take orders from department store and boutique buyers. With the foot traffic they're expecting, it was too good a chance to pass up."

"Besides," Sadie said, "no one will be coming to the store while the fair is on."

"Good point," Liz said. "Well, I'll leave you to it. I'm going to the bank."

She made quick work of the errand and, on the way back, decided to stop at Sweet Everything, the bakery next to the inn. Its owner, Naomi Mason, was part of the Material Girls stitching group along with Liz, Mary Ann, Sadie, young nurse Caitlyn Ross, and the sweet Opal Ringenberg.

Bells jingled over the door as Liz entered, and the delicious scents of chocolate and vanilla drifted to her nose. At this time of morning, only a few patrons were scattered at the small tables set against soft gray walls.

"What's good today?" Liz called to Naomi, who was busy emptying a tray of freshly baked éclairs into the case. The attractive bakery owner was about Liz's age, with dark curly hair and brown eyes.

"Everything!" That was Naomi's standard reply. She set the tray on the back counter and smiled at Liz. "How are you?"

"Great, thank you," Liz said. She paused to study the case's delicious offerings, which included cakes, cookies, scones, muffins, and pastries. "I have almost a full house this week. People are in town for the Amish craft fair." She thought of John Smith. "Well, most of them, anyway."

"I know. It's been busy here too." Naomi gestured at the case. "I've had to bake second batches of everything."

"I'm glad you did," Liz said. "I don't have time this week to bake for coffee hour." She offered the social event every afternoon at the inn so guests could relax and mingle. "And I might buy some of those peach streusel muffins for breakfast too."

Naomi smiled. "Don't they look scrumptious?" Still wearing gloves, she opened a box then reached into the case. "Half a dozen?"

"That sounds good. And I'll take a dozen each of the chocolate chip, double chocolate, and oatmeal cranberry cookies too."

As Liz paid for her order, she noticed a flyer taped to the counter below the register: "Please support the Transitional Housing for Families Project."

"What's that?" she asked Naomi.

Naomi handed Liz her change. "Some friends and I are banding together to fix up an apartment house for homeless families. They can stay there for up to a year while they get on their feet. The apartment house was donated, and we just need to renovate it. A local organization is going to run it for us."

Liz felt a pang at the thought of families without homes. She'd seen plenty of men and women on the streets of Boston, and it had always broken her heart. "Are there a lot of homeless people around here?"

The baker looked grave. "More than you would think. And the sad thing is, about half are children."

"That is terrible." Liz took one of her bills and stuffed it into the jar on the counter. "I want to help in some way."

Naomi grinned. "That's what I was hoping you would say. I'd like the Material Girls to paint some of the interior during one of our meetings. We can always use a break from stitching, right?"

Liz picked up her purchases. "Sounds like a great idea. Let's do it." One of the many things she enjoyed about Pleasant Creek was the sense of community and caring. As she left the bakery, she decided to take a look at her books again. Maybe she could squeeze out a larger donation for the project. Liz smiled. The best part about success was the opportunity to give back.

––––––– ⁄⁄⁄⁄⁄⁄⁄⁄⁄⁄⁄⁄⁄⁄⁄⁄⁄⁄⁄⁄ –––––––

The summer evening was slowly shading to night as Liz drove away from the inn, headed for dinner with Jackson. Since their destination, the Lakeside Inn on Crystal Lake, was a bit of a drive away, they were meeting at Cross Furniture Company. According to Jackson, he and his team had been working around the clock to get ready for the Amish fair.

As she traveled along the quiet streets, elbow on the window ledge, enjoying a warm breeze on her face, Liz smiled. The day had gone well, with three women, including a middle-aged pair of friends, checking in after John Smith. That left one room vacant after a cancellation. But with the fair getting underway the next day, she anticipated it would be snapped up quickly.

As Liz slowed to park near the furniture store, a gray sedan came roaring away from the curb toward her. As he rocketed past, Liz glimpsed a balding man with glasses at the wheel. He didn't even glance her way as he passed within inches of her car.

Shrugging off the incident, she parked near Jackson's sedan and shut off the engine. As she got out of the car, she heard voices through the office's open windows. Jackson and another man—tall with a dark ponytail—were talking in the office. She walked toward the steps, then hesitated, not sure if she should interrupt.

"I can't believe you called OSHA on me." Jackson stood with hands on hips, his expression thunderous.

Liz paused. *Uh-oh. Should I leave?*

Before she could move, Jackson went on. "You know I run things up to snuff. He didn't find a thing, did he?" He ran a hand through his hair. "I don't need this right now. Things are tough enough with losing that big order."

Instead of empathizing with the business owner or apologizing, the other man sneered. "It's part of my responsibility as foreman to make sure we're complying with regulations. And I wasn't sure." He stood with fists clenched. A nasty smirk flitted across his face. "I'm still not. Maybe you paid that guy off."

A series of emotions ran over Jackson's face at the man's words. Shock, confusion, and then anger. "All right, that's enough." He jabbed a finger at the door. "You're fired."

The man reared back and shouted, "I'm not fired! I quit!" He glared at Jackson. "You'll regret this, Cross!"

2

The man stormed across the office, yanked the door open, and disappeared from view. Moments later, he burst out of the store, the keys on his belt jingling. Up close, she noticed he wore cowboy boots, jeans, and a work shirt with sleeves rolled to the elbows, revealing tattooed forearms. Barely sparing Liz a glance, he headed for a battered black pickup truck parked nearby. The motor started with a throaty rumble and he was gone, the truck jouncing onto the main road.

Jackson appeared in the doorway, a rueful smile on his face. "I'm sorry you had to witness that, Liz. Not a pretty situation."

"I understand. Employee issue?" Liz was sympathetic. Although she had wonderful employees at the inn, she knew from experience that difficult situations often came with the turf.

"Exactly." With a headshake, he pulled the door shut and locked it. "I wanted to show you some of our latest pieces, but let's wait until another time. After the day I've had, all I want is a relaxing meal with good company."

"Me too." Liz smiled at the mayor, casual yet elegant in his outfit of an open-collared white shirt and dress slacks with polished loafers. "My car or yours?"

"I'll drive," Jackson said. He went around and opened the passenger door of his car for Liz with a sweeping gesture. "Your chariot awaits."

Liz slid into the seat, enjoying Jackson's courtly manners. Getting to know him had been one of the best things about moving to Pleasant Creek. Although she wasn't eager to get into another relationship like the one she'd had in Boston, she looked forward to their occasional outings.

Jackson started the car and soon they were driving along a country lane toward Crystal Lake. "Have you ever been out here?" he asked. "Although the lake is small, there are numerous cottages, a motel or two, and a beach."

"No, not yet. I've heard it's lovely." Liz studied the landscape unfolding beyond her window—pastures and woods and farms set among rolling hills.

"Lakeside Inn is a landmark. I thought that, as an innkeeper, you'd enjoy seeing the operation." He raised his eyebrows, teasing. "Even if they are rivals."

Liz laughed. "I always check out the competition. And if I can eat good food along the way, all the better." Liz had made a point of investigating other bed-and-breakfasts when she could, both in Indiana and beyond. Along the way, she gained lots of innovative ideas and, at times, learned what not to do.

"Speaking of competition, I'll have some at the fair," he said with a grimace. "Several other furniture companies are attending."

"I'm sure yours will rise to the top," Liz said loyally. Jackson's company produced beautiful, simple furniture in the Amish style. She'd bought a few of his pieces for the Olde Mansion Inn.

"Thanks for saying that, Liz." Jackson's gaze was warm. "A big order or two wouldn't come amiss. It's been a tough year."

The road narrowed and Liz glimpsed blue water through the trees. Her heart quickened as they approached the resort area, marked by an increase in both foot and vehicle traffic. Families strolled, eating ice cream or lugging umbrellas and coolers as they made their way from the sandy beach.

Jackson slowed to a near crawl and trolled along the waterfront, careful to stop at crosswalks. "The inn's a little farther, on the right."

Liz noticed the flags and flower beds first, then the pleasant white-frame building with its glassed-in wraparound porch. A sign read, *The Lakeside Inn. The Clegg family—serving your family since 1946.*

"It's lovely." Liz noted rambling wings and a backyard patio as Jackson pulled into the drive. "It's bigger than it looks at first."

Jackson found a parking spot. "According to Alfred and Doris, the owners, they've been growing steadily. That wing was new a few years ago."

Will I ever need to add a wing? Nope. Her inn was the perfect size now for her to manage comfortably.

A paved path lined with flowers led to the front door, which opened into a spacious lobby with a low, beamed ceiling. A middle-aged man presided behind the registration desk, his attention on paperwork. Dressed in a striped shirt, bow tie, and suspenders, and sporting a curled mustache, he resembled a Victorian-era gentleman.

"May I help you?" he asked automatically as they crossed the carpet. When he recognized Jackson, the man came around the desk to greet them, hand outstretched. "Jackson! Where have you been?" He pumped Jackson's hand vigorously. He turned to Liz. "And who's your charming companion? You've been holding out on me." A gold filling winked when he grinned.

Jackson put an arm around Liz's shoulders, ushering her forward. "This is Liz Eckardt. She owns the Olde Mansion Inn in Pleasant Creek. Liz, this is Alfred Clegg, proprietor of this fine establishment."

Alfred chuckled. "Don't let Doris hear you say that. She's the real boss." He reached out to shake Liz's hand. "Nice to meet you. I've heard many good things about your place. Welcome to mine."

"It's beautiful." Liz glanced around, admiring the overstuffed chintz furnishings, polished floorboards, and Persian carpets that gave the place a relaxed, comfortable ambiance.

"Two for dinner?" Alfred asked. At Jackson's affirmative, he led them to the large dining room off the lobby. "Take extra good care of these folks," he told the young woman behind the hostess podium. "They're friends of mine." He winked at Liz. "Enjoy."

The hostess escorted them to a prime table next to a window overlooking the lake, then placed menus on the table with a promise that their server would be right over.

"What a nice man," Liz said as Jackson held out a chair for her.

"He sure is," Jackson said as he took his own seat. "He and his wife give a lot of money to charity." He picked up a menu and pointed out an entry to Liz. "I recommend the steaks. They're sourced from a local farm."

Liz decided to splurge. Without lingering over the other tempting offerings, she set her menu aside. "That sounds perfect. I'm starving."

The server soon bustled over, bringing them water with lemon and taking their orders. Along with steak—medium rare for Jackson and medium for Liz—they chose mashed potatoes, fresh green beans, salad, and iced tea.

By the time their salads arrived, the dining room was almost full. At each table the waitstaff had lit candles, which glowed around the room, reflecting in the plate-glass windows. Soft classical music played. Liz found herself unwinding, content to be in the moment.

Jackson gave a sigh as he forked up lettuce. "I needed this break. Everything has been so hectic over the last few weeks. In addition to building furniture for the show, I've had to help coordinate everything with county officials and governments in other towns and cities. This event is a huge effort for all concerned. We're expecting thousands of visitors. And at least a hundred vendors."

"Mary Ann and Sadie will be among them," Liz said. "They felt it was worth closing Sew Welcome to go." She popped a cherry tomato in her mouth. As the juicy bite released its flavor, she thought of her own garden. *Poor Kiera and the mystery of the chomped tomato.* She laughed and Jackson gave her a curious look. "Sorry," she said, dabbing her mouth with her napkin. "We had an animal munch our prize tomato in Keira's garden today." She told him the story.

He grinned. "Animals like them as much as we do." He took a final bite of salad and set his bowl aside. "Here comes our meal."

The smell of sizzling steak drifted to Liz's nose when the server set the platter in front of her, making her mouth water. She picked up her steak knife and fork, and cut into the thick, tender meat, releasing streams of juice. Across the table, Jackson was following the same ritual, a look of anticipation on his face.

Then he dropped his knife with a clatter, startling Liz. His gaze was fixed on the dining room door. He craned his neck, muttering, "What is he doing here?"

Jackson's ex-employee stood in the dining room doorway talking to Alfred, and by their angry faces and clenched fists, Liz could tell the conversation was tense. The hostess swiftly moved away from the podium, hurrying toward the kitchen. *To get help, perhaps?*

When Alfred moved to block the man's entrance into the dining room, Jackson gave a grunt of disgust. Throwing down his napkin, he stood. "Excuse me for a minute, will you, please? I'll be right back." He strode across the dining room, shoulders squared.

From her seat, Liz watched the unfolding scene with concern. Had the dark-haired man followed them here? But why? To cause a scene? It didn't make sense.

The three men moved away from the opening and out of sight at Jackson's urging, but even across the crowded dining room with its clatter of silverware and soft conversation, Liz heard a bellow, followed by a shout. Heads turned. She half rose from her seat, wondering if she should go see what was happening, but before she could decide, Jackson appeared, heading her way in a hurry. The other diners watched his progress curiously, then went back to their business.

"Sorry about that—again." Jackson dropped into his seat and pulled up to the table. "Did you ever do something that you thought was a good idea only to figure out later it was a terrible mistake?" He picked up his knife and fork, and sawed at his steak.

"Once or twice. We all have." Liz deliberately made her voice soothing, hoping that he would be able to calm down and enjoy his well-deserved dinner.

He took a bite. After he swallowed, he said, "I wasn't going to talk about this, but I really need to get it off my chest." He gave Liz a straight-lipped smile. "I hope you don't mind."

"That's what friends are for. Please, go ahead if it will help." Liz reached for a roll and buttered it, giving him time to collect his thoughts.

He glanced around to be sure no one nearby was listening. "When the man you just saw, Horace Henry, showed up on my doorstep a few weeks ago, I thought he was a godsend. One of my foremen was out after an operation and we were short-handed, especially with the fair coming up. He claimed to have experience in furniture making so I took him on." He shook his head. "I'll never be so hasty again."

"But it's understandable. You were in a bind," Liz said. "Was his work okay?"

Jackson nodded. "His ability and productivity were never the problem. He's a fine craftsman. But he was edgy and argumentative with the other men." He rolled his eyes. "Only when I wasn't around of course. Typical bully. Finally, one of my most mature and reliable woodworkers, Jedediah Borkholder, came to me in confidence. You know, Miriam's brother-in-law." He paused. "Apparently Horace made a habit of spewing unpleasant slurs against the Amish. The others confirmed it when I asked."

"That's awful." Liz cringed. She detested religious prejudice—in fact, she hated bigotry of any kind. In addition, most of Jackson's employees were Amish, and Horace's attitude must have made the work environment unbearable.

Jackson sighed, his shoulders slumping. "Tell me about it. But then it got worse. Horace actually called OSHA on me, claiming we had violations." He gave Liz a tight-lipped smile. "Do you know how stressful that is, even when you're doing everything right? The man didn't find anything, thankfully. They can be really strict."

"Why would he do that?" Liz was puzzled by Horace's adversarial behavior.

"I think to get back at me. He wanted a raise, but I said no. And I had it out with him last week about how he was treating the men."

The server appeared at Jackson's elbow. "Everything all right here? Need anything?"

"We're all set," Liz said. "I'll take coffee later." The young woman bustled off.

"So I had to fire him." Jackson shook his head. "Not pretty."

"And then he turns up here." Liz pondered the situation. "Do you think he's going to continue to make trouble?"

"I sure hope not. I hope word about the OSHA inspection doesn't get out. That kind of rumor can kill your business, even if it's not true." He looked down at his barely touched meal and laughed. "Literally. But enough of all that. Let's enjoy our dinner." He picked up his fork and dug into the potatoes and gravy. "Yum. These are awesome."

"They sure are." Taking her cue from Jackson, Liz let the issue of Horace Henry go and changed the subject. "You know how they say pets resemble their owners? Or vice versa?"

Jackson looked Liz up and down. "Fortunately that's not true in all cases. You and Beans?" He shook his head. "I don't see it."

Liz laughed. "Thank goodness. Though he is a cutie in his own way. Anyway, today . . ." She related the arrival of John Smith and his basset hound with its selective hearing. Jackson laughed in appreciation when he heard how the dog wouldn't come when called.

By the time dessert arrived—apple crisp with homemade vanilla ice cream—their moods were light, almost buoyant. "I can't believe I'm eating this," Liz said, spooning up the last bite of rich, spicy apples. "I'm so full."

"Me too," Jackson said. "But sometimes you just need dessert." He set his dish aside. "Want to take a walk by the lake to burn off some calories? The path is lit."

"I'd love to." Liz reached for her purse, intending to split the bill but Jackson waved her off.

"My treat. After all, you did have to deal with all my drama." He opened the guest-check holder, ready to insert his credit card. His brows lifted. "There must be some mistake."

"Did they overcharge?" If so, Liz was surprised. All the staff here seemed very competent.

Jackson waved for the server. "Quite the opposite. Alfred gave us a complimentary meal."

Liz was stunned. "I can't accept that."

"Me neither." Jackson slid his card into the slot and handed it to the server. "Please go ahead and run this." At her startled protest, he added, "I'll take care of Alfred later."

"Before we leave, I need to make a visit to the ladies' room," Liz said.

"Go on ahead. I'll meet you in the lobby."

Jackson was lingering by a rack of tourist brochures when Liz emerged from the restroom. "Ready?"

Liz nodded, casting a curious glance at the front desk as they passed. Alfred was nowhere in sight; instead, an older woman was working on the computer.

"Goodnight, Doris," Jackson called. He gave her a thumbs-up. "Great meal, as always."

The woman glanced up with a smile. "Glad you enjoyed it, Jackson. Come visit us again." Her once-over of Liz was curious but friendly. Liz waved good-bye in return.

Outside, the evening was still warm and fragrant scents drifted from the extensive flower beds. Along the road, people were strolling or sitting on the porches of motel rooms and cottages visiting. At one end of the village, Liz spotted the bright lights of a merry-go-round and several other rides.

"This is very festive," she said. "Something for everyone."

"Isn't it great?" Jackson ambled along beside her on the wide sidewalk that bordered the road. "I used to love coming out here as a kid."

They spent a pleasant half hour wandering through the resort. Liz even took her sandals off and walked barefoot across the warm sand. Jackson, sitting on a picnic table, laughed when she dabbled her toes in the chilly lake water and squealed.

"Come on, beach girl," he called, his voice warm with affection. "I've got a big day tomorrow."

"And I've got guests." Liz slipped her shoes back on. "Thankfully I bought muffins for breakfast so I can sleep an extra half hour." She congratulated herself on her forethought.

Soon after, they were in Jackson's car and on their way back to Pleasant Creek. By mutual accord they were silent, the only sound soft music on the radio. Beyond the car window, Liz watched the countryside flash past, lighted windows shining in the dark like beacons of home.

She thought of the homeless families, and her heart twisted in anguish. *How terrible not to have a place to call your own . . .*

Jackson slowed for a tight corner, his sedan handling the challenge with ease.

Headlights flashed brightly as they came out of the curve—on their side of the road.

3

"Jackson! Watch out!" Liz cried, shrinking back against the seat. As the headlights continued toward them, she prayed silently but fervently that somehow they could avoid an accident.

Beside her, Jackson stayed calm, expertly slowing as he edged their vehicle toward the side of the road. But to Liz's horror, she saw the shoulder was extremely narrow in this spot, with a steep drop-off into a ditch. If their wheels slid into that gully, they might flip over . . .

"Come on, come on," Jackson muttered. "Get in your own lane, buddy."

At the last minute, the other vehicle swerved back onto the other side of the road, and as it roared and rattled past, Liz recognized Horace Henry's truck. "Jackson, that was—"

But before she could finish her sentence, another set of headlights shot toward them, traveling at twice the speed limit. Jackson slowed even more and edged a little closer to the shoulder. One tire hit sand and the sedan lurched toward the ditch. Jackson lifted his foot from the gas pedal and gently tugged at the wheel, attempting to guide the car away from the soft banking.

The second vehicle zoomed past, making the sedan rock with the force of its passing. Jackson, pulled the car back on the firm pavement and hit the gas, bringing them up to speed in a hurry. "Let's get out of here before we run into any more crazy drivers." He pulled a handkerchief out of his pocket and dabbed at his forehead. "Whew. That was a close one." He threw Liz a rueful smile. "Sorry about that. Are you okay?"

"It wasn't your fault. You handled it beautifully. I'm sorry I panicked." Liz hesitated. Should she mention her belief that it was Jackson's ex-employee who had almost caused the accident? With a sigh, she decided she had to tell him. "Jackson—"

"I know what you're going to say. Horace Henry is the one who almost killed us." Jackson's tone was grim. "I don't know what his problem is, but I've had just about enough of him." He thought for a moment. "In fact, I'm going to report him for reckless driving. Who knows—maybe he's been drinking."

A little further up the road, Jackson found a safe place to pull off and made the call. He slid his phone back into its holder on the dash. "I know I had to do that, but it doesn't feel good." He shook his head. "Why can't Horace get his act together? There's a good man in there somewhere."

Liz was impressed with Jackson's kindness. "Who knows? Maybe having the police stop him will be good. Before he hurts himself or someone else."

Jackson gave a great sigh. "I hope you're right." He wiggled his shoulders as though casting off his distress. "Let's not let it wreck our night. I had a great time."

"Me too." Liz flipped through the radio channels until she found some cheerful jazz. Using the music as a launching pad, she changed the subject. "Did I ever tell you about my trip to New Orleans?"

The rest of the trip passed in a flash, and after retrieving her car at the factory, Liz headed home. A short while later she was profoundly grateful to pull into the inn's driveway. "A hot shower and bed for you, my girl," she said, talking to herself. "Big day tomorrow." The Amish fair was starting and she wanted to get inn business taken care of early so she could go over to the fairgrounds.

Liz grabbed her purse, hopped out of the car, and headed up the walkway. Then she stopped short, her breath catching in her throat.

A tall, lanky figure leaned against the wall by the front door, head down, kicking one foot back and forth, and whistling softly.

Straining her eyes, Liz stared at the figure, unable to see the man's face due to shadows from the dim porch light. He wore jeans and a work shirt, just like Horace Henry. But why on earth would Horace come to the inn? Unless he thought Jackson was coming here too. The idea of his former employee stalking Jackson gave her chills.

Then the man broke out into song, his deep gravelly voice singing "The Yellow Rose of Texas" in a thick Texan twang. The light hit his face and Liz saw he had a buzz cut and hawk-like features. Relief rushed over her. Definitely not Horace. But who was he?

Bracing herself, Liz strode boldly forward. "May I help you?" she called, attempting to make her tone friendly but firm.

The man straightened fully. "Hey there, little lady. Are you the proprietor of this fine joint?"

"I am. Are you looking for a room?" Liz reached the steps. "I happen to have one open."

He gave a whistle. "Thank goodness for that. I'm about dead on my feet. I've been driving for the past two days."

Liz unlocked the door. "Are you here for the fair?" She headed inside, leaving the door open for her guest.

"Fair? Oh—yeah, that's right, I'm here for the fair." He followed her to the front desk, where a lamp was burning.

As Liz booted up the system, he leaned forward, resting his elbows on the top of the counter. A faint odor of spicy cologne and tobacco emanated from him. He idly picked up a flyer for the craft fair.

"Are you interested in furniture?" Liz asked, sliding a registration form over for him to fill out. "I have a friend who makes excellent pieces."

"Furniture?" He cleared his throat. "Yes, I'm interested in furniture.

I, um, buy a lot of it." He grabbed a pen and filled out the sections with a loopy scrawl. He pushed the form back to Liz.

"All right, Mr. Dunn. How long will you be staying with us?"

"As long as it takes." At her disconcerted reaction, he guffawed. "Sorry about that, ma'am. I'm a joker from way back." His eyes darted to the flyer. "Put me down for a week for now. Oh, and call me Tommy."

"And I'm Liz." She took his credit card and ran it, then printed the reservation for him to sign. "We're all set, Tommy. If you'd like to get your luggage, I'll show you upstairs."

He fetched a duffel bag from his car and returned. Liz grabbed the key and took him upstairs to the Heirloom Room. She unlocked the door, flipped on the light, stood back—and winced.

Tommy Dunn stepped inside, a comical look of amazement flashing over his face. The Heirloom Room was furnished in white and blue, a frivolous confection of a space with its four-poster canopy bed, Tiffany lamps, lace pillows, and carved fireplace. In contrast, large, masculine Tommy with his bowlegged stance resembled a bull in a boudoir.

"Uh, Liz . . . this is . . ." He dropped his duffel, waving a hand at the frills and furbelows.

"Feminine?" Liz bit her lip. "I'm sorry, but this is the only room I have left. If you want to cancel—"

"No, I'll stay." He poked his head into the bathroom. "It's nice, even if it isn't my style." His grin was wide and cheeky as he hooked his thumbs in his wide belt with its big brass buckle. "I prefer something a little more rustic, like my ranch house."

Liz almost asked if he was a cowboy but refrained. Instead she merely said, "I'll let you get some rest. Have a good night."

"Good night, Liz. Sleep tight."

"You too." As she closed the door, she heard him start whistling again, fortunately at a very low volume. The rest of the bedroom doors were firmly shut, and the last thing she wanted was complaints about noise from guests. Nowadays, people splashed their thoughts—both good and bad—all over the Internet. So far her ratings were uniformly high, and she wanted to keep it that way.

The next morning, despite her resolve to sleep in a little, she was up at six. Satisfying and delicious meals were a big part of a bed-and-breakfast's reputation. Since she was up, she decided she would make an egg-and-mushroom casserole with link sausages on the side. Along with those, the peach muffins and bowls of yogurt with blueberries would complete the spread, providing an array of choices.

After dressing, she made her way to the kitchen. Here she found Beans and his new friend, Rover, waiting by the dog dishes. "What are you up to, boys?" Liz filled Beans's dish with kibble while the other dog looked on with mournful eyes.

"Where's your owner, Rover? I don't think he'd appreciate me feeding you." Dog dietary needs were almost as varied as those of humans nowadays. Thankfully Beans thrived on basic kibble with a few treats thrown in.

She did give Rover a dish of water and he lapped thirstily, along with Beans, making her chuckle. After washing her hands and making coffee, she went to the pantry to pull out the box of peach streusel muffins.

Beans trotted over, tags jingling, and looked up at her, his tongue lolling out. "No muffins for you, Beans" Rover joined him. "Or you."

The back doorknob rattled and John Smith entered, garbed in sweatpants and a Windbreaker, a bandanna tied around his forehead. "Good morning, Liz."

Liz returned the greeting. She gestured to the muffin box. "Would you like a muffin and coffee?"

He strode over to the table and peered at the box. "Absolutely not. I never eat muffins." He patted his ample belly. "I'm trying to lose weight, hence the jogging, painful as it is. Now if you'll excuse me, I'm going up to shower." At the kitchen doorway, he whistled and Rover trotted to follow him.

Liz put the muffins on a plate and carried them out to the dining room. She hoped the other guests weren't on diets. Beans gave a gentle woof and Liz laughed. "I know you're not on a diet, Beans. Don't worry."

Tommy Dunn was first to appear at breakfast. The gangly Texan heaped his plate with eggs and sausage, and sat down to tuck in.

Elaine Windsor and Brenda Harris, the 50-something friends, came down next. To Liz's amusement they were wearing similar outfits—pastel polyester pants, flowered blouses, and matching cardigans secured by sweater clips. Elaine had a dark bob and Brenda's hair was blonde and permed.

Brenda waved a cheery hello while Elaine said, "Good morning, all. Isn't it a lovely day?" The duo spotted the Texan and hastened to sit one on each side of him.

"I'm Elaine." She held out her hand to Tommy.

"Tommy," he said, shaking her hand gently.

"And I'm Brenda." She nudged Tommy so he turned to her for a handshake. "What are you doing in Pleasant Creek?"

Tommy's head swiveled back and forth between the women. "I'm, ah, here for the show. The one with furniture."

Elaine squealed, clasping her hands together. "You are? So are we."

"We're on a buying trip for our gift shop in Sioux City, Iowa." Brenda scooped a tiny helping of eggs and plopped it on her plate.

"I'm from Houston," Tommy said. "Texas."

"As if we couldn't tell by your accent," Elaine simpered.

"Coffee?" Liz asked, brandishing the pot.

"Yes, please." Elaine held up her cup. "Thank you."

Liz poured coffee for the women and refilled Tommy's cup. As she turned to go to the kitchen to brew more, another guest, Dolly Craven, appeared in the doorway. Tiny, curvy, and blonde, she wore her hair in a beehive that added five inches to her small stature. Although she had to be over forty, judging by her laugh lines, she had the vibrant demeanor of a much younger woman.

"Mornin', y'all. Is there anything left or did you scarf it all up?" Dolly gave a tinkling little laugh. She sashayed over to the table and took the seat directly opposite Tommy. Resting her chin on one hand, she batted her lashes. "And who are you?"

"This is Tommy," Elaine said. "He's here for the show."

"He's from Houston, Texas." Brenda looked him up and down. "Where do you work, by the way? I wonder if I've heard of your store."

Without answering, Tommy's gaze ricocheted from woman to woman, his shoulders shifting in discomfort. Noticing Liz holding the empty coffeepot, he pushed his chair back. "Let me help you."

The three women gave good imitations of disgruntled cats as Liz hurried out to the kitchen, Tommy on her heels.

On her way to the sink to rinse the empty carafe, Liz pointed to the coffee station, where a fresh pot waited. "Not much to do, as you can see."

Tommy drew a deep breath as he glanced around the kitchen. "I had to get out of there for a minute. I felt like I was surrounded."

"They're all nice ladies, I assure you." Liz opened the fridge. "Why don't you take some fresh cream in?" She pulled a pitcher out of the cupboard and filled it halfway.

Tommy ran a finger inside his shirt collar. "Sure, they're good-looking, but they're as nosy as calves at feeding time." He chuckled as he picked up the cream. "And I'm the grain bucket."

"Ah, they're just curious. That's part of the fun of staying at a bed-and-breakfast. Getting to know the other guests." Liz grabbed the coffee.

John had joined the others by the time they reentered the dining room, and the trio had turned their curiosity on him, Liz noted with amusement.

"So, John," Dolly drawled. "What are you doing in this little old town?"

He looked down his long nose at her as he took a serving of eggs and sausage. "I'm here on private business, madam."

Brenda leaned back and studied John through narrowed eyes, tapping one long finger on her chin. "You look familiar to me. You ever get to Sioux City?"

John laughed. "Can't say I've had the pleasure."

"Elaine, doesn't he look familiar?" Brenda asked. She turned back to John. "I know I've seen you somewhere."

"I have one of those faces," John said. "People are always saying that to me." His tone was still light, but his features tightened in annoyance.

As Tommy sidled back into his chair, Dolly gave John a rest and focused on the Texan once more. "I heard you're in furniture. What do you think of this sweet little antique I bought?" She thrust her phone at him. Liz, passing along pouring coffee, glimpsed a picture of a beautiful desk.

Tommy gave the photograph a few seconds. "Very nice."

"Let me take a look," John said. Dolly passed him the phone. Pulling out a pair of reading glasses, he studied the photograph, zooming in on the details. With a curled lip, he handed the phone back, pointing to a close-up picture. "That's a reproduction. See the screws? Modern." At their curious glances, he added, "I've furnished a home or two with antiques. I had to learn to spot the fakes so I didn't get fleeced."

"Well, shoot." Dolly's expression was crestfallen. "I knew the price was too good to be true. I know toys, not furniture. I own Dolly's Toy Box in Chicago."

"Cute name," Tommy said, helping himself to more eggs.

Brenda's eyes were bright. "As I was telling Tommy, we're here to look for items for our gift shop. I understand there will be some gorgeous baskets available."

"And quilts," her friend said. "No one quilts like the Amish."

"You'll have to look for the Sew Welcome booth," Liz said. "Did you notice the shop here in the inn? The owners will be at the fair with lots of quilts and other stitched items made by Amish women."

"We did see it and were disappointed it was closed," Elaine said. "We'll be sure to look for their booth."

Liz finished serving coffee, asked if anyone needed anything else, and headed back to the kitchen. There she found Kiera, standing uncertainly inside the doorway.

"Good morning. Would you like to have some breakfast?" Liz liked to feed the thin young woman every chance she could.

"I will in a minute, thanks." Kiera hesitated. "But first, can you please come check the garbage? It looks like something—or someone—got into it."

4

Liz followed Kiera out to the shed, where wheeled municipal trash cans and recycling bins were stored. At first glance, everything looked normal. "What are you talking about, Kiera?" Liz asked.

"Look." She flipped the lid on the trash can. "I noticed the mess when I brought a bag out here." She pointed to a tied bag sitting on the garage floor.

Liz peered into the can. The top garbage bag was torn open, the contents spewing out. Keira showed her the other can, where she saw the same thing.

"How did it get inside?" Liz asked.

Keira looked sheepish. "I left the shed window wide open last night. Remember, I was airing out the place? Whatever it was took advantage. My guess is a raccoon did it. I'm sorry, Liz. It won't happen again."

"Don't worry about it. But we'll have to put that garbage in a new bag. They won't take a broken one."

"I'll do it," Keira said. "And I'll wash the can too."

"I'll help you," Liz said. Yes, Kiera had left the window open, but it could just as easily have been her. She didn't keep anything valuable in the shed, so she wasn't overly concerned. "But have breakfast first." She patted Kiera on the shoulder. "Thanks for taking such good care of the place."

Kiera beamed. "You're welcome. I love working here." She rubbed her belly. "And I love your cooking."

Liz zoomed through her morning chores, eager to get to the craft show. By the time she was done, her guests had all dispersed, heading over there themselves—all except for John, who continued to be mysterious about his plans.

Not that Liz pried. She'd learned that some guests shared everything, while others kept their business close to their vests. Either way, she just wanted them to be comfortable and make themselves at home.

Around noon, she gathered her pocketbook and a large tote bag for purchases, then stopped by the front desk. Sarah was going to watch the desk and field any calls.

"I'll be back around four or so," Liz said. "Just lock up when you're ready to leave. We've got a full house, so no one else will be checking in."

"I'll be here until three or so," Sarah said. "Then I've got to go home and help prepare dinner. Most of the family is at the craft fair with goods to sell. Miriam has several quilts at the Sew Welcome booth." Sarah's mother-in-law was a talented quilter, one of the best Liz knew.

"The show is a great moneymaking opportunity, isn't it?" Liz knew that selling handmade crafts helped many Amish families make ends meet, a welcome supplement to their farming income.

Sarah nodded, her cheeks glowing. "It is. And even better, it's bringing publicity to our work. I've heard buyers from around the country will be there. Who knows? We might get enough orders to stay busy all winter."

"That would be wonderful." Liz picked up her bags. "I'll be off, then. See you tomorrow."

The fairgrounds were outside of town, set among farms owned by Amish and English alike. Traffic grew thick on the rural road miles from the gate, a sign that the event was well attended. Liz lowered her window rather than run air-conditioning, determined to enjoy the summer day despite the delay.

Inside the gates, Liz was waved to a parking spot in a field, joining seemingly endless rows of cars and trucks. After gathering her belongings, she made the trek to the main building, in company with dozens of other fairgoers. She recognized a few faces from Pleasant Creek, waving and calling hello. Her steps quickened as she approached the doorway, suddenly eager to be part of the festive gathering.

Liz stopped to pay the modest door fee and receive a fair map from a friendly worker, identified by his red vest and Volunteer button. Once away from the crush at the entrance, she stopped to look over the map.

The show was divided into sections, with craft disciplines grouped together. The furniture was in the center, with fabric arts, candles, woven baskets and other goods, wood products, toys, and food items. In addition, another building housed a food-service area with meals and beverages.

The fabric arts were at the back of the building, so Liz decided to make a circuit around the perimeter. Her first order of business was to check on Mary Ann and Sadie. Then she would browse the various categories, her Christmas list in mind.

"Liz! Liz!" She turned to see Caitlyn Ross, the youngest of the Material Girls, trotting toward her. Perky Caitlyn, with her short red-streaked hair and pierced nose, was an emergency room nurse and one of the liveliest people Liz knew.

"Hi, Caitlyn." Liz beamed at the young woman.

"Want to walk around together?" Caitlyn leaned close to Liz. "I'm dying to buy some candles. They're my secret indulgence."

"You're in the right place," Liz said. "All kinds of hand-dipped and beeswax choices here."

They moved slowly along the aisles, stopping to examine items and, in Liz's case, making mental notes to return later. She liked to see everything before making her final selections, although she wished she had the funds to buy something from every vendor. Each booth display was a testament to hard work, talent, and creativity.

Near a display of wooden utensils, Liz spotted one of her guests. "Hello, Elaine. Are you enjoying the show?"

The other woman broke into a huge smile. "I sure am. I've found dozens of items I want to add to our inventory." She peered curiously at Caitlyn. "Hi, I'm Elaine. I'm staying at Liz's lovely inn."

"Caitlyn. Nice to meet you," Caitlyn said. Then she jumped as Brenda popped around the display suddenly. "Um, hello."

Elaine laughed. "This is Brenda, my good friend and business partner. Brenda, Caitlyn."

"Howdy," Brenda said with a nod. "Good to see you again, Liz. We were hoping to find the booth for the quilt shop you recommended."

Liz threw Caitlyn a roguish glance. "Right this way."

"Good job," Caitlyn whispered to her. "I'm sure Mary Ann and Sadie will appreciate it."

Sew Welcome had a nice corner spot, and a cluster of customers were already clamoring for assistance. Brenda and Elaine exchanged glances, then darted into the fray as one.

"I guess they don't need much help after all," Liz said with a laugh.

"It's great to see the Sew Welcome booth is so popular," Caitlyn said. "Maybe we should come back later."

"That's a good idea." Then Liz nudged Caitlyn. "Do you suppose that little boy is by himself?" A dark-haired, slender boy was hovering near the quilted purse display. Ever since Liz had adopted her godson, Steve, after the death of his parents years ago, she had had radar for little boys who appeared to be vulnerable. Steve was an adult now and serving in the military, stationed in Kosovo, but that hadn't turned off Liz's mom instincts.

Caitlyn studied the customers nearby. "It sure looks that way."

The other patrons appeared to be ignoring him, stepping around him as though he wasn't there.

Liz hesitated. Was she overreacting? Then she decided it was better to be safe than sorry. "Let's go talk to him and find out where his parents are," she said.

She and Caitlyn hurried over to the display. On the way, they spotted Chief Houghton of the Pleasant Creek police department at another booth.

"Why don't I get the chief, just in case?" Caitlyn asked.

"Good idea." Liz put a warm and hopefully nonthreatening expression on her face as she approached the boy. "Those are pretty purses, aren't they?" She studied him closely, noticing big brown eyes, freckles on a pug nose, and close-cropped hair. He wasn't dressed in expensive clothes, but his overalls and T-shirt were clean.

"I like this one." The boy pointed to a cheerful design of yellow sunflowers. "My mom will like it too."

"Is your mother here?" Liz asked.

The boy shrugged. "She's around here somewhere. But don't call her. I want to buy her a surprise present."

Liz checked the price tag. *Quite a stretch for a child.* "The purse is really expensive."

"I know. But it's okay." He fished in his pocket and, to Liz's amazement, pulled out a hundred-dollar bill.

Chief Houghton and Caitlyn approached, both noticing the denomination with surprise. "Young man, that's a lot of money," the chief said.

The boy's brown eyes filled with fear and he took a step back. "I . . . I . . . it's mine!" he yelled, then turned and darted away.

The chief made a halfhearted attempt to give chase, but quickly abandoned that idea. "I'll never catch him. He's fast." He shrugged.

"Sorry to scare him off that way. But how many kids do you know who carry around a Ben Franklin?"

"Maybe he earned the money mowing lawns or something," Liz said. But judging by his size, he wasn't more than seven or eight. *Too young to be wandering around alone.*

Caitlyn stared into the crowd. "I sure hope he finds his parents."

Houghton shuffled his feet. "Tell you what, I'll tell the security team to keep an eye out for him." He hesitated. "And I'll do a circuit myself, just to make sure he's okay."

"Thanks, chief," Liz said. "I'm sure he's probably with his mother by now anyway." *I hope.* After the chief strode away, she turned to Caitlyn. "Actually, I'm worried sick. Do you want to look for him with me?"

"Of course. Browsing doesn't seem like that much fun right now."

The duo made their way through the entire building, stopping now and then to ask people if they had seen an unaccompanied boy. Some shook their heads, claiming not to have noticed him, while others pointed, conveying the direction he had gone.

Finally they circled back to the entrance gate, where the same volunteer said, "You just missed him. He ran outside." He shook his head. "Is he yours? You oughta keep a better eye on him. Anything could happen to a little fella in a place like this."

"We know," Liz muttered, not bothering to correct the man's impression that Liz was his mother.

As they exited through the double doors, Caitlyn said, "I don't understand something. If his mother was here, why was he still alone?"

"Good question. You'd think by now she would be broadcasting his description over the loudspeakers." That's what Liz had done once, immediately after Steve got separated from her while shopping in a mall. She would never forget the bone-deep panic she'd felt when she first realized he was gone. Fortunately, a nice security guard and a prompt announcement had led to a speedy reunion.

There was no sign of the boy outside either. As Liz surveyed the vast parking area used by fairgoers, the rows of vehicles glinting in the sun, she felt herself sag with defeat. "I guess we lost him."

"Let's check one more place," Caitlyn said. "There are some people unloading in that parking lot. Maybe they've seen him."

Liz followed Caitlyn's pointing finger to where men and women bustled around trailers, trucks, and cars parked in a paved lot on the side of the building. "Good idea. That must be the exhibitor entrance." Outside there were far fewer people, so it would be harder to miss a child.

"There's Jackson," Caitlyn said as they reached the parking lot. The mayor was walking toward a long black trailer parked along the edge of the lot.

Liz's heart lifted. "Jackson!" she called, waving as they hurried toward him.

He stopped to wait for them. "Hello, Liz, Caitlyn. Here for the show?"

"We are," Liz said. "But right now we're looking for a little boy who might be here alone." She quickly explained the situation.

"I haven't seen him, but I just got here. Let me check my trailer and then I'll help you look."

Liz's heart swelled with gratitude. She could always count on Jackson. "Thanks. That would be great."

At the trailer, Jackson went to the rear, pulling a ring of keys out of his pocket as he went. He found the right one and turned to the locking mechanism. A puzzled look flashed over his face, followed by concern. "Someone took my lock." Handing the keys to Liz, he fumbled at the latch, moving it so he could open the door. He pulled on the lever and the door swung down to form a ramp.

The inside was filled floor to ceiling with stacked furniture—tables and chairs and tall cabinets. "It doesn't look like anything is missing," Liz said, the tension in her belly dissolving with relief.

Jackson stepped up into the trailer. "You're right, everything appears to be here." He lifted the corner of a protective blanket, flinging it back to reveal a glossy tabletop.

Someone had sprayed the gorgeous wooden furniture with red paint.

The table was ruined. As Jackson began to frantically throw back additional covers, she saw that several more pieces had been spattered with scarlet paint.

"I don't believe it. Someone vandalized my furniture," Jackson said. He put both hands to his head and groaned. "This is a disaster."

"I'll go get Chief Houghton," Caitlyn said. She ran toward the building, shoes clattering on the pavement.

Liz stepped further into the trailer and helped Jackson uncover the rest of the furniture they could get to. The damage was confined to the pieces in the rear, which the vandal could easily reach.

"Maybe it can be removed," Liz said. She scraped at a blotch with a fingernail. It peeled off and she held the chip up for his inspection. "See? It scrapes off without hurting the wood."

"That's good news, but it will take hours to fix this. And everything will have to get a new topcoat." Liz could tell the wheels were already turning in Jackson's head.

She placed her hand on his forearm. "Don't let whoever did this win," she said. "Your furniture needs to be in this show."

"You're right. Thanks, Liz." Jackson pulled his cell phone out of his pocket and punched buttons. "I'm going to call the shop. They can put what they're doing on hold and fix this for me today." He placed the call and gave his shop foreman a quick rundown. "I'll take this trailer back to the shop to unload," he said to Liz as he hung up. "I'll also get some other pieces from the warehouse to fill in." He shrugged. "They're not my favorites, but they'll do in a pinch."

Chief Houghton appeared in the doorway, Caitlyn at his heels. "What's going on, Jackson?"

Jackson showed him the damage. "Someone broke in here and spray-painted my furniture."

"Any idea who could have done it?" Shaking his head, Houghton bent to examine a table leg, scraping it with his thumbnail much the way Liz had.

The mayor pressed his lips together. "Maybe. I hate to make accusations though." He stepped down the ramp a couple of steps and studied the building. "Are those cameras working?"

Chief Houghton joined him, staring up at the eaves where cameras were placed. "I can find out. The security team here is in charge of that."

"Let's go do that now. Then I'll head back to the factory." He glanced at his watch. "With any luck, I'll have my display done this afternoon."

In the excitement, Liz had almost forgotten about the little boy. While following Jackson and Chief Houghton into the building, she and Caitlyn stopped and asked a few other people if they had seen him. Finally, a man unpacking boxes of baskets said he'd seen him hugging a woman, who then had headed with him to the visitor parking lot.

"That doesn't sound like a kidnapper," Caitlyn said. "I think he's okay."

"I hope so," Liz said. She still couldn't shake the feeling that something was a little odd about the boy and his situation. As the chief had pointed out, how many children carried hundred-dollar bills around?

Inside the venue, the chief led the way upstairs to an office that overlooked the main floor. Here several security officers were watching cameras. These displayed views of the entrances, places around the floor, the hallways to the restrooms, and the food court.

"We have a situation in the vendor area outside," Houghton told the head officer, an African-American man with a friendly face and close-cropped hair. "One of the trailers was broken into."

The man swiveled around to face them. Liz noticed his nametag read *Ronnie*. "I'm so sorry to hear that. What happened?"

Jackson stepped forward and outlined the problem. "The trailer was fine when I left it here yesterday afternoon around three. So it must have happened sometime between then and this morning."

Ronnie picked up a pen and tapped it on the desk. "People were working here until about ten o'clock last night. And they started up again real early, probably at six." He called to a woman across the room, "What time did you get here, Darlene?"

"About six. I unlocked the vendor entrance myself." Darlene shrugged. "I didn't notice anything out of place."

"The only sign was the missing lock," Jackson said. "And the spray-paint damage was confined to the interior of the trailer."

Ronnie swung around to his desk. "Let's look at footage from last night. Maybe we'll catch this guy. Or gal."

The group clustered around his desk as Ronnie deftly selected the right camera and brought up the relevant footage. "You're in luck. All this gets erased after twenty-four hours unless someone reports an incident."

Ronnie set it on fast-forward so the digital numbers in the corner whizzed through. For several long minutes, nothing happened on the video footage. Then something changed.

"Aha. There he is." Ronnie stopped the feed, setting it on regular speed.

While Liz watched, heart in her mouth, a figure wearing a hooded jacket crept toward Jackson's trailer. He or she set down a sack, pulled out bolt cutters, and made swift work of Jackson's lock. This went into the sack. The door was unlatched and the person moved inside, carrying the sack. A few minutes later, the person reemerged, shut the back door and slouched away.

"Well, there's proof something happened," Jackson said. "Can't we zoom in on that person any better than that?"

The security officer shook his head. "I'm afraid not. Did you check for prints?"

"No, not yet." Jackson groaned. "I probably smudged them."

"Don't beat yourself up," Caitlyn said. "You were in a panic to open the trailer—and rightly so."

Liz noticed something on the video. "Run it back. I think whoever it was used a sleeve to open the door so they wouldn't leave any fingerprints."

She was right. The crafty vandal had pulled the long sleeve over his hand like a mitten and used it to open the latch and pull the door down, and then had performed the reverse when leaving.

The group stared at the video in silence for a long moment.

"I'll file a report with you, chief," Jackson finally said. "But I'm not going to involve my insurance company—or the fair's—since that will gum up the works further. I have to get the furniture cleaned up and back here today."

"Fair enough," Ronnie said. "We'll take pictures so you'll have them for a claim if you do one later. Darlene will go down with you." He turned to another man seated nearby. "Let's get another camera installed at the vendor entrance today. And extra people on patrol tonight." He shook his head. "I hope we don't get a repeat with you or any of the other exhibitors."

Jackson gave an ironic chuckle. "They won't hit me again. I'm going to be locked up tighter than Fort Knox."

Down in the exhibit hall, Jackson headed off with Darlene to photograph the vandalism. Liz watched them go, wishing Jackson had taken her up on an offer of help. But he'd assured her that his employees would be able to handle everything.

"What do you want to do now?" Caitlyn asked Liz.

"I'm not sure." Liz glanced around the hall full of enticing offerings, not caring about them in the least. "I'm all out of sorts after the situation with Jackson. And that little boy."

"Me too." Caitlyn ran a hand through her hair. "How about we get coffee and something chocolate, and then we'll swing by the Sew Welcome booth?"

"Sounds good." Liz scanned for the sign leading to the food court. "Coffee's that way."

In the food court, another large hall ringed with booths, they were surprised to discover Naomi tending a Sweet Everything booth.

"I didn't know you were going to be here," Liz said. She studied the bakery case, trying to decide between a double chocolate brownie and a blondie frosted with chocolate.

"I didn't either," Naomi said. "But the opportunity came up late yesterday when one of the vendors pulled out. One of my employees is at the shop in town, and I've got another baking up a storm." She gestured at the case. "I've sold tons already, more than enough to offset the fee."

"I'm sure you have. The place is packed." Liz tapped a finger on her lips. "Sorry, I'm having trouble deciding."

Caitlyn nudged Liz. "Let's get one of each and trade halves."

"Great idea," Liz said. She placed the order for the treats and two medium coffees, house roast. Then she noticed a familiar flyer. "Caitlyn, Naomi is on a committee that is creating housing for homeless families."

The other woman read the flyer, tutting in concern. "Count me in." She foraged through her handbag and stuffed a couple of bills into the jar.

"Don't worry, I will. The Material Girls are doing a painting day," Naomi said. "That is, if I can convince the others."

"Piece of cake," Caitlyn said with a smile, picking up her coffee and the plate holding the brownies. "We'll go ask Mary Ann and Sadie after we eat."

Activity around the Sew Welcome booth had slowed enough that Liz and Caitlyn didn't feel like they were interrupting when they hailed their friends.

"How's it going?" Liz asked. "We came by earlier, but you were swamped."

Mary Ann folded a set of place mats. "We haven't had a chance to catch our breath. Not only have we sold a lot of inventory, we've also taken several orders from stores."

"I wasn't so sure about attending at first," Sadie admitted. "But it's paid off. Not just in sales but exposure too. If I had a dollar for every person who's told me, 'I didn't know you were in Pleasant Creek,' I'd be a rich lady."

"Good idea to print these flyers." Liz picked one up. "Thanks for the plug."

It read, *Visit Sew Welcome, located at the Olde Mansion Inn, in lovely downtown Pleasant Creek.* Several photographs, including one of the inn, made the flyer eye-catching and attractive.

"Have you two done a lot of shopping?" Mary Ann asked. She moved on to another set of place mats, these ones with the sunflower fabric the little boy had admired.

"Not really." Liz filled them in about the little boy, and then she and Caitlyn told them about the vandalism to Jackson's furniture.

Mary Ann gasped. "That's horrible." She glanced around at their stock, as though imagining it sprayed with paint. "Thank goodness the furniture can be cleaned. All of our cloth goods would have been totally ruined."

"Any idea if he was targeted, or was it random?" Sadie asked. "I haven't heard anyone else complain about being tampered with."

Liz moved closer to the counter, not wanting to broadcast Jackson's troubles to the shoppers milling around them. "He had a falling-out with an employee last night. So it might be personal. But still, you should be careful."

"I think we ought to keep all our extra stock in here," Sadie said, "not out in the van." She lifted the tablecloth over one side of the booth. "Most of it will fit under here."

"The security team is putting on extra people and another camera," Caitlyn said. "So they're taking it seriously."

"That's great, but it won't help once someone wrecks your stuff," Sadie pointed out. "Some of our stitched things are irreplaceable."

"We'll help you unload if you give us the key." Liz held out her hand. "That all right with you, Caitlyn?"

"Absolutely. Can we leave our bags here?"

"Of course." Mary fished behind the curtain framing the back of the booth. "We have a hand truck you can use. The boxes are kind of awkward."

They made a couple of trips with the dolly, noticing that other vendors appeared to be doing the same. Apparently the word was out about the vandalism. In the furniture area, Jackson's booth was the only one still empty, only a few pieces in place and no one there to talk to customers.

Worry knotted Liz's belly. Would Jackson's sales recover after missing most of a day?

Later that evening, Liz had assembled the ingredients for the next morning's breakfast and done her daily kitchen cleanup. After hanging up her apron, she set a step stool in front of the cabinets so she could reach her favorite cut-crystal bowl, which would be perfect for the potpourri she had purchased at the fair. A friend back in Boston had given her the piece, and she rarely used it. Here was a perfect opportunity to keep it on display.

There it is. Holding the fragile dish firmly in her grip, Liz backed down off the step stool and set the bowl on the counter. She untied the plastic bag and carefully poured the fragrant contents into the bowl. She'd set this in the library on the mantel, where it would perfume the air nicely.

While she worked, she admired the last rays of the summer sun tinting the back garden and Jaynes Lake, the small body of water behind the inn. Clouds massed in the sky above, flaming gold and red—and black?

Liz dropped the package of potpourri, scattering it across the countertop. *Something is on fire!* She ran to the back door and out into the yard, eyes fixed on the location.

Yes, a billowing column of black smoke rose above the trees. Not many buildings were in that direction, only a few houses on a dead-end lane. Liz fumbled for her cell phone and called 911. She told the dispatcher she had spotted signs of a fire.

"Yes, ma'am. Emergency vehicles are on their way," the dispatcher said.

As Liz disconnected, she heard the sounds of fire engines racing to the spot. On an impulse, she decided to go check it out. Rather than drive over, which might impede the fire trucks, she decided to take the path around the lake and cut through the woods. On her frequent walks, she'd often seen the path going that way, but had never taken it. It probably was used by residents of the side streets in that area.

Liz's feet pounded on the path, her heart racing as she hurried to the scene. What was it about fires? Although dreadful, they also aroused fascination, attracting people—including her—like moths.

She picked her way through the rapidly darkening woods, guided by flashing red and blue lights and the sounds of shouting. As she got closer, she saw surreal shadows cast by the fire and the vehicles, swarms of firemen in slickers moving about a burning house.

A house. Her belly swooped in horror. The barn standing a fair distance from the house appeared unscathed, thanks to firemen training hoses on it too.

The woods thinned, becoming an overgrown field. Liz, planning to keep well out of the way, circled the edge of the pasture, making her way toward where a cluster of spectators stood watching.

Liz's toe stubbed against something soft but firm. Only by windmilling her arms was she able to remain upright. Puzzled, she turned to see what she'd tripped over. It wasn't a rock or branch. Bending over, she pushed aside the long grass.

A teddy bear lay on the ground, its black button eyes winking in the reflected firelight.

6

Liz grabbed the toy and clutched it to her chest. She stared at the fire in growing dread. Was a child trapped in the house? She had no real basis for this thought, but the incongruous sight of a stuffed animal aroused every fearful instinct.

Changing direction, she trotted through the field toward the burning building, careful to keep out of the way of the firemen and the hoses crisscrossing the ground. The fire roared like an angry beast, crackling and snapping. A beam collapsed with a great gust of flames and sparks.

Chief Houghton stood near one of the fire trucks, his face grim as he watched the inferno. Beside him was Paul Brewster, the fire chief. In his forties, tall and muscular with blue eyes and receding blond hair, Paul was a familiar sight around town when off duty.

Liz waved the teddy bear as she ran up, shouting to be heard over the noise of rumbling engines. "Chief Houghton, Chief Brewster!"

"What am I looking at, Liz?" Houghton asked, taking the bear she thrust at him.

"I found this in the field." Liz turned toward the house, now collapsing into itself. "No one was in there, were they?" Her voice shook.

"No signs of life," Paul said. "The fire started in a corner away from the back door so if someone had happened to be inside, they would have escaped."

"And the door was open," Houghton said.

"I'm so glad to hear that." Liz pointed at the bear. "But where did he come from?"

Houghton shrugged. "Probably some kid dropped it." He handed Liz the toy.

Liz squeezed the bear and put it to her nose. It didn't smell or feel damp, as it would if it had been on the ground for a long time. "Well, it must have happened recently." She tucked it in her jacket pocket.

Jackson Cross pushed his way through the crowd, greeting the officials and Liz. "A total loss, huh?"

"The house is for sure," Paul said. "But we saved the barn."

The mayor frowned at the smoldering structure. "I wonder what happened. My employee—or should I say ex-employee—lives here. Horace Henry."

"Really?" Paul frowned. "I'd like to talk to him about the fire. But no one was on the property when we arrived."

"Who reported the fire?" Liz asked. "I called 911 when I spotted the smoke, but the trucks were already on their way."

Paul gestured up the road. "A neighbor saw the smoke too. There are only a few residences on this street, so we're lucky someone noticed it before it spread."

Houses just don't burn down by themselves. Had Horace burned down his own house? That seemed crazy. Or had he left the stove on or a lit cigarette near paper? Liz thought about asking the fire chief but decided not to butt into the investigation. Maybe Horace Henry could shed some light on the issue when they located him.

Another tall figure appeared out of the night, his eyes wide as he examined the remains of the house. "What happened here?" When he spoke, Liz recognized Tommy Dunn, her Texan guest. What was he doing here?

Paul shot him an irritated look. "That will be determined when the fire marshal does his investigation."

Tommy nodded. "I see. So it's suspicious in origin?" He seemed undeterred by Brewster's abrupt manner.

"I didn't say that. Any fire of unknown origin has to be investigated." The fire chief squared his hat more firmly on his head. "I'd better check in with my team." He stalked off.

Houghton turned to Tommy. "And you are?"

Liz stepped in. "This is Tommy Dunn, one of my guests." She introduced Tommy to Houghton and Jackson. "Tommy's here to buy furniture at the show." Liz raised her brows at Jackson, hoping he would understand the message.

"Is that so?" Jackson said, eyeing the newcomer. A warmer note crept into his tone. "Welcome to Pleasant Creek."

"Liz runs a fine establishment," the chief added. "Enjoy your stay."

"Nice to meet the local law," Tommy drawled. "And yes, this little lady does a superb job of making her guests welcome." He nodded at the house. "So what's your theory?"

"I don't have one," Houghton said. "All I know is the Clegg farm has been empty for years, and I'm surprised that house didn't go sooner. Kids like to play in there and the barn too."

Tommy started. "The Clegg farm, you said?"

Liz's interest was also piqued, as she had just met two people of the same name the previous day. "Do Alfred and Doris own it?"

"The innkeepers? No. An uncle, I think. The place is in pretty poor shape, so no one's wanted to live there, as far as I know."

"Except my employee," Jackson said. "This is the address he gave me. I guess he didn't mind roughing it." He and Tommy stared at the charred building, wearing almost identical expressions of suspicion. Liz understood Jackson's interest, but why did Tommy care beyond the usual curiosity displayed by a bystander? For a furniture buyer, he certainly seemed interested in a fire investigation.

Shrugging off her fruitless speculation, Liz said, "I'm headed back to the inn. You're welcome to come over for coffee, any and all of you."

"Thanks, Liz," Houghton said. "But we'll probably be here all night. We have to wait until the fire has burned down enough to leave the site."

When she got back to the house, Liz put the kettle on. After witnessing the fire, she needed the comfort of a hot drink, even if it was still over seventy degrees outside. Her guests were home, with the exception of Tommy Dunn, and she decided to see if anyone wanted a bedtime snack.

She started with the third floor, where John and Rover had retired. Both doors were open, allowing her a view of John doing a headstand in the middle of his room. She tried to back away, but he spotted her and brought his feet down onto the carpet.

"I'm sorry," she said. "I didn't mean to interrupt." Rover lifted his head from his supine position on the carpet and woofed softly at Liz.

"No problem," John said, his face beet red with effort. "I had reached my limit."

"I came up to see if you'd like hot cocoa or tea. I've also got decaf coffee. And cookies."

"Cocoa sounds nice, if I can have it with skim milk and artificial sweetener." John reached out and stroked his dog's head. "Would you like a bedtime snack?" Rover moaned in delight. "I'll take that as a yes."

"See you in a few. We'll be in the four-season room." Liz scooted down the stairs to the second floor. Dolly was getting ready for a bath, so she declined. Down the hall, the Rose of Sharon Room's door was ajar. Brenda was staying in there, she remembered. As she neared the room, she heard voices.

"We didn't do too badly," one woman said.

The other laughed. "Not at all. And it's only the first day."

They must have found some good products to buy. Liz lifted a hand to knock just as Elaine opened the door wider, preparing to leave her friend's room.

"Hi, Liz. Can I help you?" Elaine asked.

Feeling uncomfortably like she'd been intruding, Liz said, "Sorry to bother you. I came up to see if you'd like cocoa and cookies. Or tea. John is coming down."

The friends exchanged glances. "What about that Texan?" Brenda asked. "Is he going to be there?"

"I'm sure he will. He's out right now, but I expect him back any minute." In fact, Tommy had told Liz he'd be over shortly when she'd left the Clegg farm.

"Cocoa sounds great," Elaine said. "Give us a minute."

"Of course." Liz hurried toward the staircase, feeling once again that she had done something wrong. She wasn't quite sure what.

Downstairs, Liz prepared a pot of hot cocoa and set mugs and a plate of gingersnaps on a tray. Beans snuffled around at her feet and she gave him a dog treat. "Your friend is going to be coming down," she said. She laughed at herself. Who would have guessed she would be fussing over a bulldog as part of her daily routine? *Far better than the legal beagles I dealt with during my law career.*

John and Rover were already in the four-season room when Liz entered, Beans at her heels. The dogs immediately greeted each other by touching noses. Liz and John shared a chuckle at the sight.

"I'm glad Rover made a new friend," John said. "I like him to have a healthy social life."

"I guess dogs need friends too." Suppressing an eye roll, Liz set the tray on the table. She loved her pet, and he was part of the family, but in her opinion, some people went overboard.

"Of course they do." John ruffled Rover's long ears. "They're pack animals." He sat back in the rattan chair with a sigh. "What a nice place you have here."

"Thank you." Liz handed him a cup of hot chocolate. "I strive to make my guests comfortable, and I'm happy you're enjoying your stay."

John blew on the cocoa and took a tentative sip. "We are. Rover slept really well last night. I think I only heard him get up once." He took another drink. "He usually has insomnia."

That is an endorsement! Liz toyed with adding it to her brochure. Beans, now prostrate on the rug, chose that moment to give a loud snore. "I don't think my dog has that particular problem," she said dryly.

Brenda and Elaine bustled into the room, their eyes lighting up when they spotted John. They swooped to sit in chairs flanking him and, after getting settled, glanced up at Liz expectantly.

"That looks good," Elaine said, glancing pointedly at John's mug of cocoa. "Do you have whipped cream?"

"Coming right up." Liz poured them each a cup and added generous helpings of whipped cream. "Not everyone likes whipped cream. That's why I waited."

"We don't count calories," Brenda said, taking the cup with a nod. "Do we, Elaine?"

Her friend patted a trim midsection proudly. "No, we're too busy running around to gain weight."

"I envy you." Liz held out the plate of cookies. To her amusement, both refused while John took several, despite his earlier concern about his weight.

"Did you hear about the vandalism at the fair, Liz?" Elaine's eyes were wide.

Liz perched on a sofa with her drink. "You mean what happened to Jackson?"

Elaine waved a hand. "I don't know his name. Someone's trailer was broken into, that's all I know. A lot of dealers were upset."

"Jackson Cross's furniture was spray-painted inside his trailer," Liz said. "But I think he'll be able to fix it."

"What type of furniture does he make?" John asked.

"Wooden pieces in the Amish style," Liz said. "He's got a website if you're interested. Cross Furniture Company."

Brenda pulled out a phone. "Let's look it up." She soon found the site, then handed the phone to Elaine.

"This dining room set is gorgeous." Elaine passed the phone to John.

"The furniture is all wood and solidly built," Liz said, feeling like a salesperson. But if it helped Jackson recover from the setback, she was happy to do it. "He has Amish craftsmen working for him, and they do an excellent job."

John examined the website, commenting on various pieces as he scrolled. He especially admired the four-poster bed and matching bureaus in rustic cherry.

"Are you in the market for new furniture?" Liz asked boldly. "I can introduce you to Jackson." Her heart beat a little faster at the thought of closing a deal. Maybe being a salesperson wasn't so difficult after all. Of course, craftsmanship like Jackson's sold itself.

"I might be." John shrugged. "I keep my eyes open for nice things wherever I go."

"You should come to the fair, see everything in person," Brenda said. "I've never come across so many wonderful crafts in my life."

"The place was mobbed," Elaine said. "We could barely move."

John looked sheepish. "I actually was there for a while this morning.

I found some beeswax candles to use for dinner parties. But as you said, it was hectic, and Rover gets nervous in crowds." He reached down and patted his dog's head. "Don't you, boy?" The dog regarded him adoringly, then flopped his head back onto his paws.

"A dog that gets nervous? I never heard of that before." Elaine darted a look at the hapless mutt. "Maybe he needs medication." She cackled.

Liz thought of adding that Rover also suffered from insomnia but held her tongue.

Brenda nudged her friend. "Hush. Some people are sensitive about their pets' . . . issues."

John sat bolt upright, offended. "My dog doesn't have issues. He's a very intelligent animal and, as such, is sensitive to his surroundings." The curl of his lip conveyed an unflattering opinion about Rover's present company.

Uh-oh. How am I going to smooth this one over? Liz was searching for words when she was saved by Tommy Dunn's arrival.

He stepped into the room, bringing a strong scent of smoke with him. The others turned to stare. "Sorry," he said with a laugh, plucking at his pants leg. "I must smell terrible. I just came from that fire a couple of streets over." He paused. "The fire marshal said it was arson."

7

The women stared at Tommy, identical looks of shock on their faces. "Arson?" Brenda asked. "In a quaint little town like this?"

Tommy hitched up his pants, adjusted his huge belt buckle, and sauntered across the room to a seat. "You'd be surprised at the crime in small towns. They often give cities a run for their money."

At his nod, Liz poured Tommy a cup of cocoa from the steaming pot, her mind whirling. Someone had burned the house down deliberately. But why? And who? It couldn't possibly be worth much under an insurance claim. Had Horace done it, or was it malicious mischief—teenagers playing with matches or something similar?

Elaine shook her head. "I guess you're right. First vandalism at the show and then a fire tonight. What's going to happen tomorrow?"

Her friend elbowed her, emitting a peal of laughter. "Good question." She glanced around and gave a mock shiver. "I hope we're safe in our beds."

Liz's spine prickled, not liking the direction of this conversation. Fortunately, John piped up. "You're being a bit of an alarmist, ladies. We're out of harm's way here." He cocked a brow at Liz. "We have locks on the doors and smoke detectors, right?"

"Of course," Liz said. "You're perfectly safe as my guests." She crossed her fingers under the table, thinking of other incidents that had happened at the inn. Surely the women weren't involved in any mysteries of their own. And John was just a kindly, if somewhat eccentric, man on vacation, right? Although Liz wasn't quite so sure. The man's name, for example. It was so . . . generic.

As for Tommy Dunn, she was also having trouble getting a read on him. He claimed to work for a retail business, but something didn't ring true. He set down his mug of cocoa. "What's this about vandalism?"

"Oh yes, you might be interested since you want to buy furniture." Brenda paused for effect. "Someone damaged a trailer full of fine furniture right outside the showroom!"

"Really? Don't they have security?"

"They do," Liz said. "But the camera didn't pick up much detail." As the others stared, she added, "Jackson is a friend of mine, and I was there when we reviewed the video."

"I'm fascinated by all this modern technology," Brenda said. "Do they have many cameras on the floor?" She turned to her sister. "I'd think they'd want to protect the goods inside too, wouldn't you?"

"Absolutely," Elaine said. "There must be millions of dollars' worth of stuff in there." She twisted one of her rings absently as she spoke.

Liz thought back to when she was in the security office. Several of the monitors showed crowds surging around the booths, blocking any view of merchandise. "I'm not sure. I saw a couple of feeds, but there were so many people it was hard to see anything in particular."

"That's not good. Glad we don't have a booth." Brenda yawned widely, throwing her arms in the air. "I'm off to bed. I want to get an early start." She shook a finger at Elaine. "So no sleeping in tomorrow."

Elaine's eyes widened comically. "Me? You're the lazy bones." Squabbling in a friendly way, the two got up from the table and headed for the hallway.

John sighed in the quiet that settled after the remaining group heard the sound of doors shutting upstairs. "Those two are certainly bundles of energy."

"I hear you," Liz said, collecting the used cups. "I wish I had a fraction of their oomph."

"Thanks for a nice evening, Liz," John said. He rose to his feet and whistled. "Come on, boy, let's go to bed."

Liz stooped to give Rover a pat as he trundled past on his short legs. "Good night. Sleep tight and don't hesitate to let me know if you need anything."

Tommy drained his cup and stood, then gathered some dishes. "I'll help you, Liz. Then I'm going to take a walk around the block before turning in myself." As they dropped their load in the kitchen, he leaned toward her and whispered, "Actually, I'm going out to secure the perimeter. Don't wait up." He headed out the back door.

Liz paused in the act of loading the dishwasher. *That was an odd thing to say, "secure the perimeter."* If asked, she couldn't say who was the strangest. Tommy with his focus on security and lack of knowledge about retail, or evasive John Smith with his pile of cash. If working as an attorney—and running an inn—had taught Liz anything, it was to notice when something was off. Then she shrugged. As long as they paid for their accommodations and didn't make a mess, whatever they were hiding wasn't any of her business.

Was it?

⁓

"Which color do you think we should pick?" Sadie spread out the array of paint chips for Liz to study. "Naomi told me to get white, but now I'm getting a brain cramp after looking at all these shades." She and Liz were at the hardware store picking up supplies for the apartment they were painting that evening.

Liz scanned the dozen choices, the names reflecting the imagination of the designers. Which was better, Cotton or Cloud? Clotted Cream or Venetian Lace? Finally she waved down the clerk. "Could you please help us?"

The young man came over with a smile, and after a few pertinent questions, he gave a recommendation. "This is a very livable color, clean and clear without being too stark. If you get the satin finish it will also be easy to clean."

Liz and Sadie exchanged glances. "Sounds good to me," Sadie said. She placed the order for wall and trim paint, then leaned on the glass-top counter with a sigh. "If it wasn't for a good cause, I'd just as soon crawl back into bed right now."

"You must be tired," Liz said. "The show was really busy yesterday."

"And even more hectic today." Sadie sighed again and shifted her position. "But I can't complain. We made tons of sales."

The clerk returned, lugging a couple of gallons of paint. "Are you exhibiting at the Amish crafts show? I hope to get over there tomorrow." He set the paint on the counter.

"I'm one of the owners of Sew Welcome," Sadie said. "We sell quilting supplies and quilted items as well."

"Cool. I'm sure my girlfriend will check out your booth when we go." He moved to the cash register. "Do you have all the brushes and rollers you need?"

"Do we?" Liz asked Sadie.

"Yes, Naomi got those already," Sadie said. "We're all set."

"I'll ring you up then," the clerk said. He gave them the total and Sadie paid, one of her contributions to the project. As he handed her the slip, he leaned forward across the counter, glancing both ways. "Be careful at the show, ma'am. I heard one of the vendors was robbed."

"You mean the vandalism on the furniture yesterday?" Sadie asked.

He shook his head. "No, ma'am. One of the candle sellers reported money missing. My girlfriend works at the bank and she heard about it from a customer this afternoon."

"I guess we'd better be on the alert," Sadie said to Liz as they left the store. "It's really disconcerting to hear about the theft on top of the vandalism."

"I agree. I guess you have to be careful everywhere, especially in large crowds." To give Sadie a break, Liz had pushed the cart outside. She paused to survey the huge parking lot full of vehicles. "Where did you park again?"

Sadie pointed. "See the Ping-Pong ball on that antenna? That's where I am." She laughed. "Even my pink Jeep is hard to spot sometimes, believe it or not."

"I see it now, behind that van." Liz aimed the cart in the right direction. "It's too bad my Acura doesn't have an antenna. I'm always forgetting where I park."

They loaded their purchases into Sadie's Jeep and headed for the apartment house. The blue Victorian-style house with porches and a garage in the back was located on a side street near a park and the elementary school.

"This is nice," Liz said as Sadie pulled into the wide driveway. By the cars parked near them, Liz noticed that Naomi, Mary Ann, and Caitlyn were there. Opal was probably riding with Mary Ann.

"The absentee owner wanted to get rid of it. He was only halfway through the renovations so it's been empty a while. He finally decided to eat the cost and donate the place to a good cause."

Liz opened her door and slid down from the high seat of the Jeep. "Is there still a lot to do?" She knew from her own experience that maintaining a large building was costly.

"Fortunately, the work he did included the heating-and-cooling system, plumbing, and electrical." Sadie grinned. "All Naomi's group has to do is the cosmetics."

Liz hefted one of the gallons of paint. "That is fortunate." As she followed Sadie up the path, she thought about the families who would soon call this place home. Making it nice for them was going to be fun.

Inside the spacious hallway, with its gracious curving stair, a door to the right was open. Naomi came to greet them. "Just in time. We've just finished cleaning and prepping."

Mary Ann rose from the hardwood floor with a groan. "It's been a while since I've done woodwork. I've forgotten how tough it is to work on your knees."

Opal grinned. "Wait until you get to our age, right, Sadie?"

"That's right," Sadie said. "But if you don't use it, you'll lose it, I always say."

Smiling at the banter, Liz set her can beside a can of trim paint. She gazed around the big double room, with its bay windows, one in the front and one on the side. "Living room and dining room?"

"Exactly," Naomi said. "Let me give you the tour."

"We already got one," Caitlyn said, prying open a can of paint. "I'll give this a stir while you look around."

"We painted these rooms a few days ago," Naomi said, leading them through a good-sized kitchen done in yellow, a teal bathroom, and two bedrooms—one ivory and one blue. The smell of fresh paint still lingered. "All we need to add are window treatments and it will be ready. Then we'll move on to the other two apartments."

Liz glimpsed a grassy yard circled with trees through the windows. "What a lovely place, Naomi. Your families are going to be very happy here."

Naomi colored with pleasure. "I hope so. Who says charity accommodations need to be grim and utilitarian?"

Sadie snorted. "Like a Dickens orphanage, you mean? People are already down on their luck—you don't need to depress 'em too."

"Exactly." With a swing in her step, Naomi led them back to the front rooms. "I've got pizza coming in two hours, so let's see how much we can get done." Under her able direction, the team got to work, and by the time the delivery car pulled up in front, they were done.

"Next time I redecorate, I'm hiring you all," Liz said. "Working together, we're pretty formidable."

"I'll say," Caitlyn remarked. A smudge of white adorned her pert nose. "We're a real team." The doorbell rang and she hurried toward the hall. "This one is on me."

Naomi shook her head. "I was going to pay but I guess she won't let me."

A few minutes later they sat down in the hallway to eat, perching on the stairs with slices of pizza and bottles of iced tea or soft drinks. The exercise had made Liz hungry, and she bit into the cheesy mushroom-and-olive pizza with gusto, flavors of oregano and tomato bursting in her mouth.

"Yum," Caitlyn said. "This hits the spot."

Everyone munched in silence for a few minutes, with occasional interjections of "Please pass me a napkin," or "Would you like another piece?" Finally, each one leaned back against the step behind her and heaved a sigh of contentment. The front door stood open and they enjoyed the summer evening for a moment.

Liz spotted a young woman walking along the sidewalk. She paused to look at the house and, apparently spotting them inside, made her way up the front walkway to the porch.

"Someone's coming, Naomi," Mary Ann said.

Naomi got up, wiping her hands on a napkin, and went to the front door. "May I help you?" she asked, her voice friendly.

The woman hesitated, a look of uncertainty crossing her pretty features. She wore her thick dirty-blonde hair in a ponytail, and she was dressed in ragged jeans and a T-shirt. "I'm . . . I'm not sure. Is this the apartment building for homeless families?" She blinked her eyes rapidly, blushing.

"Yes, it is." Naomi laughed. "Or rather, it will be soon. We're getting it fixed up, and people will be able to move in by the end of the month."

"Oh. That long?" The woman's face fell, her shoulders slumping in discouragement.

Naomi took a step forward, reaching out a hand to touch the woman's shoulder. "What's your name? I'm Naomi."

"I'm Wendy Felder." The woman's gaze skittered around the rest of the Material Girls.

"I'm Sadie." The older woman took the lead and the rest of the group followed suit, all smiling warmly at the visitor.

"Would you like some pizza?" Mary Ann asked. "We have tons."

Wendy studied the open pizza boxes. "No thanks, I just ate. But I wouldn't say no to some water."

Caitlyn fished a bottle out of the cooler and gave it to Wendy. "Here you go."

"Are you looking for a place to live?" Naomi asked.

"I am. Me, my husband, and my son." Once again, Wendy's fair skin flushed, but her words were hurried, even eager, as if she was glad to finally share her troubles. "My husband was laid off from his job in Gary, and he wasn't able to find other work there. He had a lead here in Pleasant Creek, but it didn't pan out. Now he needs surgery." She pressed her lips together. "We basically ran out of money. I'm working a few hours a week at a big-box store, but it's not enough." Her brows rose. "If anyone of you need someone to clean, please let me know. I used to have a business doing houses and offices."

Liz ached with sympathy at hearing the woman's sad story. "Where are you staying now?" Sarah, Kiera, and Liz did most of the inn's upkeep, but maybe she could find a special project for the woman.

Wendy looked down toward her shoes, then back up into Liz's eyes. "In our car."

8

Mary Ann patted Wendy's arm. "And you have a child?"

"Yes, Austin is eight." Wendy's tone grew slightly defensive. "He's well taken care of. Bathed and fed."

"I'm sure he is," Sadie said. "But we've got to get you all into beds. Doesn't the town have a program to help, Naomi?"

"I was just about to say that," Naomi said. She pulled out her cell phone. "I'll call Jackson Cross, our mayor. We have vouchers available for rooms at the Sleepy Time Motel. They have kitchenettes too, which is handy."

A light came into Wendy's hazel eyes. "Really? That would be wonderful."

Naomi stepped inside the apartment to make her call. While she was gone, the others made small talk, asking Wendy about her personal interests, which included quilting.

"You'll have to come to one of our quilting groups at Sew Welcome," Mary Ann said. "Once you're settled, of course."

"I'd love that," Wendy said. "My mama always said there was nothing better than a quilting circle for friendship and fun."

"Your mama was right," Sadie said. "We've got a great group here in Pleasant Creek."

"Looks that way," Wendy said, smiling shyly around the circle.

"I'll have a cleaning job for you later this week," Liz said. She'd have Wendy help with a deep clean of her private living quarters, which never got the same attention as the rest of the inn.

Wendy blinked rapidly and Liz thought she spotted the glitter of tears. "I really appreciate that, ma'am."

Naomi stepped back into the hallway. "You're all set, Wendy. Meet Jackson at the motel in half an hour and he'll take care of the paperwork for you. And would you like me to put you down for this apartment? We haven't formally started taking applications, but I can put you at the top of the list."

Wendy practically swooned at this offer. Her face glowed. "I can't thank you enough, Naomi." She glanced around at the others. "All of you have been so wonderful." She sighed. "Getting a place of our own will be a dream come true. I've been praying so hard . . ."

Touched by Wendy's heartfelt gratitude, Liz felt a rush of tears in her eyes. By the blinking and fumbling for tissues that was going on around her, she guessed her friends were equally emotional.

"We're just glad we can help," Naomi said. "Come on, let me walk you out."

The visit from the homeless wife and mother lent wings to the rest of the work. Around nine p.m., Naomi declared them finished, and they began cleaning up. When they left half an hour later, the place was spotless, needing only furniture and a family to make it a home.

"How are you set for furnishings?" Mary Ann asked as they trooped to their vehicles, tired but satisfied with a job well done.

"We've been collecting donations and storing them," Naomi said. "I've got a list of what we need if you're interested."

"I am," Liz said. "I've got a few extra pieces kicking around." In fact, she had a rocking chair in the attic that was in perfect shape.

"I'll email it to you all." Naomi unlocked her car. "Good night. And ladies, thanks again. Our group really appreciates the help."

"No problem. It was a pleasure." Sadie cleared her throat when her words came out gruffer than normal. After she and Liz climbed into the Jeep, the older woman said, "Seeing that young woman made it real." She shook her head. "To think that she and her family have been sleeping in a car . . ." Her voice trailed off as she started the engine.

"I hear you, Sadie." *There but for the grace of God* . . . Liz considered herself a fortunate person, blessed with family, friends, and adequate income. She tried to be mindful of her blessings, having seen through her work as a lawyer how thin the line could be between solvency and disaster.

Come to think of it, didn't she have some extra bedding? And a little white bookcase? That would be perfect for Austin. Maybe she could even buy some books. Or better yet, give him a gift certificate so he could choose his own.

Warmed by these plans, Liz sat back in the seat, sighing as her sore back made contact with the cushion. An idea slipped into her mind. "Sadie, why don't the Material Girls foster Wendy's family? We can help make sure they have what they need."

Sadie turned to Liz, a big grin on her face. "Girl, you read my mind. This is going to be fun."

———

As Liz closed the door of her quarters, her cell phone rang. Her pulse leaped. *Who could be calling at this hour?* She dug the phone out of her purse, hurrying so she wouldn't lose the call. *Why does it always sink to the bottom?*

A familiar number appeared on the screen. "Jackson, is everything all right?"

He laughed. "At the moment. Sorry to alarm you, Liz, but I wanted you to know I got Wendy and her family settled at the Sleepy Time."

Liz sank onto the sofa and kicked off her shoes. "That's great. I'm so glad Pleasant Creek has that program."

"Me too. It only helps for a while, but at least it bridges the gap until people can find more permanent housing."

"I think Wendy is going to get the apartment we were painting tonight. Naomi basically promised it to her."

"That's good news. They seem like really good folks." Jackson paused. "I want to donate a dining room set."

Liz gasped, amazed at his generosity, even in the midst of his own lean times. "Oh, Jackson, how wonderful." She'd seen the price tag on his pieces and they certainly weren't inexpensive.

"In fact, I want them to keep the set after they move. They can only stay in the apartment so long, right?"

"I think a year or so. Enough time for them to get on their feet." In light of Jackson's troubles with the vandalism, his gift was even more notable. "How did it go with the cleanup?"

Jackson sighed, a great gust of relief. "Fine. The pieces look like new. In fact, why don't you come see them early tomorrow morning if you have time? I'd like you to pick out the set for Wendy. Then I'll have the men drop it off at the apartment house on the way back after unloading at the show."

Liz thought about this offer, rearranging her schedule in her mind. "I can do it. I'll have Sarah handle breakfast after I set up."

"Good. It's a date." He seemed to hear his words and was silent for a minute. "Well, I'd better let you go. It's getting late."

Liz wished him a good night, smiling as she disconnected. Their friendship was something she cherished, and if it headed in a romantic direction . . . well, maybe that would be all right. Some day.

Exhausted from painting and cleaning the apartment, Liz slept deeply, waking only when the alarm jangled beside her head. After lying still for a moment to clear her head and greet the day with a prayer, she got up and showered.

After feeding Beans, she put together ingredients for ham-and-egg breakfast cups. Baked in a muffin tin, these savory delights—or so the recipe called them—included cherry tomatoes and a dab of pesto. *It will be fun using produce from our garden, if we can keep the tomato bandits away.* Liz hoped Kiera's efforts wouldn't be in vain. Once they had a harvest, she'd have to make sure Kiera was invited for a meal made with her hard-earned bounty.

Sarah arrived as Liz was pulling out the muffin pans. "Sarah, can you take over breakfast? I need to go out to Cross Furniture this morning." Liz explained the nature of her errand and went through the menu.

"That is so kind of Mr. Cross." Sarah's eyes sparkled at the news. "I will see if any of my relatives would like to donate a quilt."

Liz poured water into the coffeemaker for a second pot to join the one warming. "How nice. Amish quilts are heirloom pieces."

The young woman smiled. "There's nothing like a warm, handmade quilt to make someone feel loved." She moved toward the cupboards. "Shall I set the table?"

"That would be great." Liz glanced at the kitchen clock, untying her apron. "I'm out of here. But I'll be back in time to clean up, so wait for me." Her employee was so efficient Liz was likely to return to a scrubbed kitchen, every trace of breakfast put away.

Sarah made a shooing motion. "Don't worry about it. Your guests will be well taken care of."

Outside, Liz paused to enjoy the fresh summer air and the sight of the sun stealing across dew-spangled grass. Birds chirped in the trees lining the street. *The soundtrack of summer,* Liz thought fancifully, then winced. *Along with that racket.* A few houses down, a lawn mower started—a neighbor probably hoping to get a jump on an unruly lawn before work.

What passed for rush hour in Pleasant Creek was just beginning, cars sharing the road with delivery trucks and vans, but Liz made it to the factory with ease. Even at its worst, Pleasant Creek's traffic was a drop in the bucket compared to the day and night roar of Boston. *Another reason to enjoy living here.*

Through the building's open windows, Liz heard the grind and whine of woodworking equipment. As she parked near the office entrance, Jackson pulled in behind her. She got out and waited for him to emerge.

"You beat me," Jackson said with a smile, jingling the office keys. "Come on in."

She followed him up the short flight of stairs and waited for him to unlock the door. "Come on in," he said, flicking on the office light. "Would you like coffee?"

"Sure, I'll have a cup." Liz looked around the small, neat office, which held a couple of desks, several file cabinets and a small kitchenette area. Near the front window was a small round table holding brochures and one potted plant.

"Have a seat at the table," Jackson said. As Liz chose a chair, he filled the carafe and poured water into the coffeemaker. A tall Amish man entered the office through a rear door. "Good morning, Jedediah."

"Good morning, boss." The man's curious gaze fell on Liz. "I'm Jedediah Borkholder, Jackson's new shop foreman."

"Nice to meet you." Liz stood to shake his hand. "I'm Liz Eckardt. Your sister-in-law, Miriam, is my cousin."

Jedediah returned the handshake with a firm, work-worn grip. "Pleased to meet you too. I think I've seen you at some of the large family gatherings."

"How are things going on the floor?" Jackson asked. He pulled several mugs out of a cabinet and filled them with steaming java.

"Humming along smoothly. Of course the men were upset to hear about the vandalism, but I've managed to help them channel their anger into being extra productive."

"Thanks. I don't know what I'd do without you." Jackson's tone was heartfelt.

"Glad I could help." Jedediah added cream to his mug. "By the way, Chief Houghton called and said he would be swinging by this morning. Think he knows who did it?"

"I hope so," Jackson said. "That was really unnerving. It makes me glad we put in a security system."

"Everything looked fine here this morning." After chatting with Jackson about the day's orders—a fascinating glimpse into the company's workings—he excused himself to go back into the shop.

"Are you ready to pick out that dining set?" Jackson asked.

Liz drained her cup and stood. "Sure am."

Jackson gave Liz a set of earplugs and safety glasses, and led her into the workshop. Inside, it was noisy and smelled pleasantly of sawdust. Liz gazed around curiously at the men working at various stations. They cut wood, shaped pieces, and assembled beautiful furniture. Jackson paused at several spots to explain what was happening. Cross Furniture sourced all the wood here in the United States, Jackson explained, making it a truly American product.

At the far end was the shipping area and, adjacent to that, a small showroom displaying pieces of furniture and portable samples, chair legs and drawer fronts in various finishes.

Jackson pointed out a couple of tables, one in a rich cherry finish, the other golden oak. "I've discontinued these styles, but I've got one or two sets left, which I'd usually sell at a discount. I'd like to donate one."

Liz thought about the apartment, trying to picture the furniture in place. With its bay windows and tall ceilings, the oak set would look right at home. The table had four chairs with a scroll back design.

She reached out and stroked the satiny surface. "This one is perfect."

Jackson beamed. "That was easy."

Jedediah strolled into the sample room. "Find anything you like?"

"All of it," Liz said. "You do beautiful work."

"Thank you. It's an honor to carry on the tradition of Amish craftsmanship."

Jackson patted the tabletop. "Liz, will you let me know the address and a good time for drop-off? Jedediah, we're going to donate this set. Can you get it ready for delivery?"

"Sure thing." Jedediah peered out the window. "The chief is here."

Rather than go back through the factory, Jackson took Liz outside through another exit. "Chief!" He waved to get Houghton's attention as he exited his car. "We'll be right with you."

The trio met at the cruiser and went into the office. "Coffee, Chief?" Jackson asked.

"I would like a cup, thanks." Houghton sat at the table, joined by Liz. "Going out to the fair today?"

"Yes, I am. Sadie and Mary Ann need my help. They didn't realize how busy they would be."

The chief sighed. "It is going well, in that aspect. But with the vandalism and one of the vendors being robbed, the security team has their hands full. So we're lending officers. Me included."

"Any leads on who broke into my trailer?" Jackson asked as he delivered a cup of coffee to the chief.

Houghton shook his head. "Not yet. I wanted to talk to you again and see if you had any ideas." He spooned sugar into his mug and stirred. "It might have been random, but it seems to me you were targeted deliberately." He took a sip. "Feels that way with the theft too. Someone knew that vendor had lots of cash on hand."

Red bloomed along Jackson's cheekbones. "I agree." He pressed his lips together, obviously warring with himself. "Look, I hate to say this, but I think you need to investigate one of my former employees. We parted on, shall we say, bad terms a couple of days ago."

The chief's gaze was level. "You fired him?"

Jackson shifted in his seat. "I had to. Look, chief, I really hate to get into the details. Suffice it to say Horace Henry's termination was well-deserved."

Houghton's mouth hardened. "Did you say Horace Henry, as in the man who was living at the Clegg farm?"

"That's right. Bad things seem to follow Mr. Henry."

A vehicle entering the yard caught Liz's eye. She watched as a sedan pulled up to the building and two men got out, both carrying clipboards. One was balding and the other had a crew cut. "Looks like you've got company, Jackson."

Jackson rose to his feet and peered out the window. "I'm not expecting anyone."

The two men climbed the steps, footsteps thumping, and banged on the door. Liz, sitting closest, said, "I'll get it."

The bald man flashed an identification badge at her. "We're from OSHA. Here to do an inspection."

Behind her, Jackson muttered, "How nice. Horace Henry's legacy lives on." He pushed back his chair and joined Liz. "What's this about? The inspector who was here the other day said everything was fine."

The man sporting a crew cut gave Jackson a smile. "Follow-up, strictly routine. But it'd be best if you cooperate." As he waved the arm carrying the clipboard, Liz noticed he had a tattoo on his hand that ran up under his sleeve. *I suppose even government officials sport those nowadays.*

"Come on in then and get it over with," Jackson said. "I'll join you." The bald man started to protest, but Jackson put up a hand. "That's my right."

As the men stepped inside, Liz saw one hesitate when he passed Chief Houghton. But at Jackson's gesture both continued on inside.

"I'll get out of your way, Jackson," Houghton said. "Come down to the station later and we'll talk." He tucked the pad into his jacket pocket. "Right now I've got to go out to the fair. Doing extra duty out there this week." With a tip of his hat, he left.

"I'd better get going too," Liz said. "See you later, Jackson." She sent him a look of commiseration. "Hang in there." It couldn't be pleasant having federal inspectors go through your business, even if you were following regulations.

"Thanks, Liz. I appreciate your support." His shoulders slumped as he turned to the waiting men. "Right this way, gentlemen."

As Liz trotted down the steps, headed for her car, she said a little prayer for Jackson. Letting a bad employee go seemed to have made things worse, not better, for the business owner and mayor. A lot worse.

9

"There you are!" Mary Ann greeted Liz with a smile when she arrived at the Sew Welcome booth a couple of hours later.

Liz stepped behind the table, raising her voice to be heard above the noise in the exhibit hall, which was almost deafening. If possible, even more people were attending than the previous days. She'd even seen the two OSHA officials who had visited Jackson among the shoppers. "Have you been busy?"

Mary Ann nodded. "Insanely busy." Leaning close to Liz, she whispered behind her hand, "The woman Sadie is waiting on has a store in Indianapolis. She wants dozens of our bags. We'll have to hire Miriam and maybe some other stitchers to make them for us." At the other end of the booth, Sadie was conferring with a middle-aged woman examining the quilted totes and handbags.

"Wonderful. Can we go through the procedure to ring up sales?" Liz watched as Mary Ann demonstrated how to use the credit card reader and showed her the cashbox.

"Believe it or not, a lot of the customers have been paying in cash. We're not taking checks. At the store we send them through the reader like a debit, but we're not set up for that here." Mary Ann frowned in concern. "I hope this all makes sense."

"I'll be fine. Besides, Sadie is still here. Go get some lunch before you drop." With a laugh, Liz shooed her tired friend out of the booth.

Standing behind a booth was like resting in the eye of a hurricane, Liz decided. People swirled around her. A familiar figure appeared in the crowd, her guest John Smith and his dog. She waved and he changed direction, heading her way.

"I see you decided to check out the fair," Liz said. "Do you like it?"

John glanced over the quilts on the table. "It's all very nice. I've been impressed by the quality."

Liz lifted up the corner of an especially pretty blue-and-white quilt in a chain-and-knot pattern. "How about this queen-size quilt? It'd look good in a bedroom."

"Hmm." John stroked his chin. "You're right. I like the simplicity of the design." He bent closer and stroked the fabric. "Such fine stitching."

"My cousin Miriam made it." Liz's chest filled with pride. It would be fun to report to Miriam that she had personally sold one of her quilts.

"She's an excellent seamstress." John reached in his back pocket. "I'll take it." He opened the billfold and pulled out a stack of money. "Would you be able to bring it back to the inn for me? I'll probably have to ship it home since I flew."

"No problem. Sew Welcome is set up to ship purchases, and as you probably noticed, the store is at the inn." Liz brought out the cashbox. *Mary Ann was right. People are using cash.* And she'd thought her guest was unusual. Perhaps not.

"Yoo-hoo! John!"

Liz and John looked over to see Brenda and Elaine approaching through the throng. Both wore beaming smiles. While Liz wrote up a receipt, the friends joined John at the counter.

"What did you buy?" Brenda asked. She pointed. "This quilt?"

Elaine fingered the fabric. "It's lovely."

Liz deposited the cash inside the box, quickly locking it and tucking it away. Then, gesturing for her guests to back up so she could reach the quilt, she wrote "sold" on the tag. "I'll bring this home with me but until then, if it's all right with you, I'll leave it here for other people to see. They might want to place orders."

"That's fine, Liz." John pocketed the receipt. Tugging on Rover's leash, he called, "Come, Rover. Let's go have lunch."

"Do you want company?" Brenda asked him. "It would be a good chance to chat. I still think I know you from somewhere."

"We were just about ready to eat ourselves," Elaine said.

John glanced back and forth between the women, looking as trapped as a rabbit between two wolves. "All right. I mean, sure, why not? Please join us."

Only a dog lover would say "us." The trio sauntered off, the friends bracketing John. "We'll be back to shop," Brenda called over her shoulder with a wave.

"Those two are really pushy," Sadie said, appearing at Liz's side.

"They are." Liz had a policy of not gossiping about guests, but she was equally astonished at the women's bold nosiness.

Sadie and Liz worked together over the next hour until Mary Ann returned. Then Sadie left, planning to run back to the shop for a few minutes and scrounge up something to eat as well.

"How'd it go?" Mary Ann asked.

Liz pointed to the stack of receipts, proud of the sales they'd racked up. "Everything is selling like hotcakes. I sold the blue-and-white quilt to one of my inn guests."

Mary Ann's brows rose. "Way to go." She quickly tallied the sales and entered them on a sheet. "We're doing even better than I expected."

Liz glanced around the booth. "I hope you have more items to put out. It's starting to look kind of bare." Indeed, the table and racks were empty in spots.

Mary Ann bent down and moved aside the tablecloth on the back table. Fishing around underneath, she pulled out a couple of large cardboard boxes. "No problem. We brought reserves."

"Good thing." Liz took the group of handbags Mary Ann handed her and hung them on the rack, careful to line them up evenly and spaced just so to display the colorful fabric patterns.

While she worked, other customers came up to browse, and several signed up for classes too. Still others took flyers and business cards. "Even if they don't buy today, we've made a contact," Mary Ann said. "That's important too."

"Hey, ladies. How's it going?" Caitlyn breezed up to the booth, scheduled to take Liz's place. She flung her purse down under the back table. "Boy, it's busy today. I had a hard time finding a parking space." The young woman looked bright as ever in white capris, a lime-green T-shirt, and matching sandals. She wore half a dozen bangles on one arm and several rings on both hands.

"Just in time," Liz said. "I'm starving." She laughed. "Not that I haven't been having fun." She tapped the stack of receipts. "I sold a ton this morning."

"And I'll try to do the same this afternoon. Maybe I'll outsell you." Caitlyn stuck out her tongue. "I'm pretty dry. Would you bring me back an iced tea when you're done eating?"

"Of course." Liz retrieved her own purse and, with a promise not to be long, aimed for the food court. The route took her past Jackson's booth, so she detoured there. He was deep in discussion with a customer, and Liz hovered nearby, waiting. The furniture looked lovely, set on platforms covered with fabric that set off the colors of the wood. Racks held brochures and catalogs. All in all, it was a very professional presentation, Liz thought.

The customer took a brochure and promised to be in touch. As the man wandered away, Jackson turned and spotted Liz, his face lighting up. "There you are. How's your day?"

"Great. I've been selling up a storm for Sadie and Mary Ann. How's it going here?"

Jackson tipped his head, considering. "Pretty well. I've had a few orders and promises of more. But so far I haven't lured in any really big buyers as I hoped."

"Give it time," Liz said. "I'm sure you'll do great."

"I hope you're right." Jackson added more brochures to the rack and straightened them.

"How did the inspection go?" Liz held her breath as she waited for the answer.

"Pretty good. They didn't find anything to write me up about. But I swear they poked their noses into every square inch of my factory."

Liz sighed with relief. "That's great news. I'm on my way to lunch. Can I bring you something?" Poor Jackson was working all alone. "I can spell you if you want a break too."

He glanced up at her with surprise. "Thanks. I was wondering what I was going to do. One of my guys is supposed to be here but he's been delayed on the road."

"Why don't I bring lunch back here to the booth? That way you won't have to wait very long."

"Even better." Jackson told her what he wanted, handing her two twenty-dollar bills. "Buy your lunch too."

"Really?" Liz held the money, hesitant. "I didn't—"

"I know you didn't. But you're doing me a huge favor."

Liz had to wait in line, but finally she was able to order two BLTs on wheat toast and three iced teas. On a whim she added chips and cookies. Manning a booth was hard work, and she for one had quite an appetite. Before returning to see Jackson, she stopped by the Sew Welcome booth and delivered Caitlyn's iced tea.

Back at the Cross Furniture booth, Jackson hurried off to the men's room and Liz settled in to eat her lunch. Hopefully customers wouldn't ask her questions she couldn't answer. That was always embarrassing.

John and Rover strolled by, the man's brows rising in surprise. "You're working over here now, Liz? You are a woman of many talents."

Liz extracted a chip from the bag with a laugh. "I'm helping my friend. He's all alone today." She waved the chip. "Go ahead and look around. I don't know much about the furniture except it's all handmade locally from American wood, with Amish craftsmanship. Really nice stuff."

"Nice stuff indeed," John muttered. He ran a hand along the side of a china cabinet. Rover exhaled loudly, reminding Liz of Beans, and plopped flat on the floor.

Liz spotted Jackson's tall figure striding through the crowd. "Here he comes now, if you want to talk to him."

John glanced over his shoulder. "Not now. I will take a brochure." He snatched one from the rack. He tugged at the dog's leash, "Come on, Rover. Let's go." To Liz he said, "He needs to go out."

In Liz's eyes the dog seemed content to lie where he was, but maybe his owner could read more into his body language than she could. She turned her attention to Jackson. "Welcome back. Not much happened while you were away."

Jackson's phone rang and he held up a finger as he answered it. "Jackson Cross." He listened to the caller, a frown creasing his brow. "Sorry, buddy, but you've got the wrong number." He disconnected and placed the phone on the table. "Some guy telling me I'd 'better come across with the money or else.'" He frowned.

"That's strange." Liz gestured at his sandwich. "There's your lunch."

Jackson picked up a sandwich half and took a huge bite. "Yum." Tomato juice dribbled down his chin and Liz handed him a napkin. He laughed. "Sorry, I'm making a mess."

"Have you ever noticed the best food is often the messiest to eat?" Liz leaned back against a table and crossed her arms.

"I never thought about it, but you're right. Take spaghetti for example. Don't eat that while wearing a white shirt. At a business meeting. Not that I know from personal experience."

"What about lobster? Once I broke open a claw and the water inside squirted my date in the face. He was sitting too close so I was kind of glad."

They traded stories about messy meals as Jackson finished his lunch. He wiped his hands on a napkin and balled up the wrapper for disposal. Standing on his toes, he aimed and tossed at a nearby can, scoring a direct hit. He shook his clasped hands in mock victory.

"If you need to go, I'll be okay." Jackson glanced at his phone as he retrieved it from the table. "My helper is due to arrive any minute now."

"I can hang out until he comes," Liz said. She shook her iced tea, making the cubes rattle. "I still have my drink left." She pointed to a small bag. "And there are cookies."

"You really know how to spoil a guy, don't you?" Jackson dove for the treat, then waved at a tall young man a short distance away. "Ah, there's Curtis, finally." He introduced Liz to his salesman before Liz excused herself.

"Liz, thanks for coming back," Mary Ann said when she returned to the Sew Welcome booth. "I was hoping you could do a deposit for us on your way home. I'll keep some cash for change but I want to put the large bills in the bank."

"Of course. The bank is on my way. And even if it wasn't, I'd go anyway." Liz smiled at her friends. Caitlyn was helping a customer while Sadie checked over forms.

Mary Ann reached under the table for the cashbox. Her brow creased in puzzlement when she set it down. "The key is still in the lock." She turned it and lifted the lid, letting it fall back. Then she cried out.

All the cash was gone.

10

"What is it, Mary Ann?" Sadie trotted over.

Lowering her voice, Mary Ann said, "Look. It's gone." Her voice held a note of barely restrained panic.

"There was a lot of cash in there," Liz said. "I made a sale that was several hundred dollars. And that was just one." Liz's heart sank at the thought her friends' earnings had been stolen. Even worse was the feeling of violation.

Sadie glanced around, eyes narrowing in a glare. "Who could have done this? Liz wouldn't have let anyone behind the table, and we sure didn't."

"No, of course not. It was fine the last time I saw it." Liz leaned closer. "Remember the candle vendor yesterday? The same thing probably happened here."

Mary Ann's face paled. "Do you think a ring of criminals is targeting the vendors?"

"Could be," Liz said. "We need to warn everyone to be on the lookout."

"After we talk to Caitlyn, let's call security and the police," Sadie said. "We need to report this." She grimaced. "And notify our insurance company." Pulling out her phone, she began to scroll through numbers.

"Let's figure out how much is missing," Liz said. "The form of payment is written on the slips."

Mary Ann took the stack and divided it. She placed a piece of paper and a pen in front of Liz. "You do one half and I'll do the other."

Liz was tallying her numbers when Caitlyn walked up, carrying several twenties in her hand. "I have a purchase but she needs change."

Mary Ann and Liz exchanged glances. "How much? We, er, have a problem," Mary Ann said.

Caitlyn's eyes widened. "What do you mean? There are plenty of fives and ones in the box."

"We'll explain in a minute." Liz opened her purse. "I've got some cash. What do you need?"

Caitlyn told her, and after writing up the slip while the customer watched curiously, Caitlyn gave her the change and sent her on her way. "What's up?" she asked. "I could cut the tension in here with a knife."

"Did you see anyone inside the booth?" Sadie asked in a low voice. "We've been robbed."

Caitlyn's eyes widened in surprise. "Seriously? That's horrible." She shook her head. "It was really busy here at times, but I don't recall seeing anyone come behind the table."

Mary Ann raised both hands helplessly. "Neither did I. I think for the rest of the fair, I'll carry any cash on my person."

"Good idea," Sadie said. "We'll get one of those money belt things." She picked up her phone and made a call. "Chief Houghton, please. I'd like to report a robbery." A security guard was strolling along the aisle nearby, and Sadie waved for Mary Ann to flag her down.

Liz recognized Darlene from the office when she and Jackson had looked at video footage. "How can I help you?" Darlene asked, hands on her hips. Her hair, pulled into a ponytail, swished back and forth as she studied each person in turn.

"Someone cleaned out our cashbox," Mary Ann said. She showed Darlene the empty container.

Darlene tsked. "You shouldn't have handled that. Now the prints will be no good."

"It was probably too late anyway," Liz said. "Mary Ann had to touch the box to discover the theft."

"Good point." The guard reached for her radio. "Base, I've got a 459 on the floor at booth E-25."

"How does she know the booth number?" Caitlyn whispered.

Darlene pointed to a nearby pole, which was adorned with a large *E* and the numbers 25–30." Her radio hissed and squawked, and she walked off a little further to talk.

"Houghton will be here in a minute," Sadie said. "He was onsite anyway."

Between crime at the fair and arson in town, the poor man is run ragged. Liz finished adding the slips and gave the total to Mary Ann, who shook her head sadly at the size of the loss.

Caitlyn nudged Liz. "Isn't that the little boy we saw the other day?"

Liz followed her gaze to two booths down, where a boy in overalls hovered near a display of packaged candy. While she watched, he picked out a box of chocolate-covered marshmallows and carried them to the woman working at the booth. In one hand, he clutched a greenback. Even from here, Liz could see it was a one-hundred-dollar bill.

Chief Houghton appeared in the crowd, spotting the boy as he handed the woman his money. He changed direction and headed toward the candy booth.

The boy's head swiveled, alternating between the candy he was purchasing and the approaching policeman, even though Chief Houghton was moving slowly in a nonthreatening way. He apparently decided to abandon both and took to his heels. The woman held up his money helplessly, staring after her fleeing customer.

"What's he afraid of?" Caitlyn asked.

"Could he be the thief?" Mary Ann's tone was doubtful. "It's hard to imagine a boy that age robbing people."

Liz did her best to follow the boy with her eyes, tracing his passage as he darted around people in the wide aisle. Where it intersected with another row of booths, he stopped next to a young woman with blond hair. She put her arm around him and led him off, but not before Liz recognized her. Before she could tell the others, Chief Houghton joined them at the booth.

"Well, that was a bust. And not the kind I like." The chief sounded disgusted. "It's kind of disconcerting to realize you scare young children." He nodded a greeting at Darlene, officer to officer.

Liz thought about telling Houghton where he could find the boy, Austin, at the Sleepy Time Motel with his parents, but she refrained. Maybe she would have a little talk with his mother first. It was odd, to say the least, that a homeless boy was carrying around a hundred-dollar bill. *Do his parents know? Where did he get it?*

"Fill me in," the chief went on. "What happened?" He took notes as Mary Ann explained, with Liz confirming the amount of money that had been in the box. Darlene offered to review security footage with the chief from the time of the last cash sale—made by Caitlyn while Liz was eating lunch—until the discovery of the missing money.

"You ought to put out an alert," Houghton told Darlene as they began to walk off. "One time is a fluke, twice is a pattern."

"We did, but we'll do it again." The security guard's ponytail bobbed as she nodded. "We've got to be careful, though. We don't want to taint the event."

"It's tainted for us," Sadie muttered under her breath.

"Now, now, Sadie," Mary Ann said. "We're covered for it. And the majority of the sales were credit or debit cards. So we're still ahead."

"I suppose so." Sadie pasted a smile on her face. "I'll be working extra hard to pay for the deductible."

"Here's our chance," Caitlyn said. "I think a bus tour just arrived." Indeed, a herd of senior citizens, all wearing similar T-shirts, was charging down the aisle. As a body, they veered toward Sew Welcome's booth, sneakers thundering.

"I'll stay for a while and help," Liz said. She felt guilty about the robbery, even though it had happened when she was with Jackson. Was there anything she could have done to prevent it? She vowed to keep a close eye on anyone who came around the booth.

As she was unlocking her car hours later, her feet sore and tired, and her cheeks aching from smiling at customers, Jackson called her cell. "Hi, Jackson. Did you have a good day?"

His voice over the line was enthusiastic. "Incredible! What a turnaround from this morning. A buyer from Chicago wants to carry my furniture in several stores around the city."

Liz paused with the door half open, pleased at this good news. "That's fantastic."

"A regular large order will keep my shop going through the seasonal lean times we experience." Jackson gave a hoot of triumph. "Want to celebrate with me? I'd like to take you to the Lakeside Inn again. Unless you'd rather go somewhere else."

Liz tipped her head back and gazed at the deep blue sky. The temperature was hovering in the low eighties, promising a balmy summer evening. "I'd love to. I've been at the fair all day though, so give me an hour to clean up."

"Sure thing. This time I'll pick you up at the inn."

Liz hung up and slid into her car. Although she'd wanted to confide in Jackson about the Sew Welcome robbery, she hadn't wanted to sour his mood. After what he'd been through lately, he deserved to celebrate a success. There would be time enough later to share unpleasant news.

All was peaceful back at the inn, Sarah and Kiera having worked their usual magic with the housekeeping and gardening. Fresh bouquets stood in the hall, on the dining table and the living room mantel, light fragrances drifting through the cool air. Kiera had also placed a few ripe cherry tomatoes on the kitchen counter with a note: *Our thief decided to leave us a few, so I wanted you to have them.* Apparently the vegetable crop continued to be pillaged by the mysterious invader.

Liz popped one in her mouth, enjoying the tart flavor, then fed Beans and retreated to her quarters for a bubble bath. Here she lit a candle and studied a couple inspirational readings, trying to center her mind. She had learned from experience that when troubles came, they usually arrived in clusters. Getting swept up in the turmoil didn't help anyone. A clear head and calm heart would be required to solve the mysteries of Horace's whereabouts, the arson, and the thefts. Not to mention the peculiar circumstance of an eight-year-old possessing large sums of money.

She took an extra deep breath of lavender-infused air. Apparently remaining calm was a bit of an extra challenge right now.

After a lengthy soak, Liz did her hair and makeup before sliding into a new navy silk pantsuit she'd been saving for a special occasion. The pants were wide-legged, swishing around her shins nicely, and the top was two-piece—a sleeveless shell and an open jacket. The doorbell rang. Liz quickly sprayed on a touch of perfume and gave her curls a final pat. Beans, who had watched her every move, grumbled at her.

"It's fun dressing up," Liz told him. "I feel like a new person." She bent and gave his velvety head a pat.

Jackson stood at the front door, holding a bouquet of white roses and hydrangea blossoms. He grinned, waving the flowers at her. "One of the fair vendors was selling these and I couldn't resist."

Liz took the flowers, burying her nose in the soft blooms. "I'm glad you didn't. They're gorgeous. Let me put these in water and we'll go." Jackson was so considerate, a real gentleman.

Soon they were on their way, on the now-familiar route to the lake. "Did I tell you I've been thinking about buying a boat?" Jackson asked. "With the new order, I might be able to finally afford one."

He began to talk about the type of small sailboat he had his eye on and how he'd always wanted one. Liz listened patiently, interjecting where it seemed appropriate. *Men and their pastimes.* Her past dates back in Boston had loved motorcycles, vintage Jaguars, and even snowmobiles. At least a sailboat was quiet.

They passed a boat launch, where several pickup trucks and boat trailers sat. "I could put in right here, even after work," Jackson said. "That's one thing I love about summer, the long days."

"Me too," Liz said. "I love being outside in warm weather."

"Well, you'll have to come out with me when I get the boat. It holds four, so we'll invite some other people along too."

Liz imagined sailing over blue water, enjoying the feel of a warm breeze in her hair and on her face. They could bring a picnic and maybe anchor near one of the small islands that dotted the lake.

Jackson slowed as he navigated one of the shore road's tight curves. In this section of shorefront, trees grew close on one side and a sheer drop-off plummeted to the lake on the other. As the road straightened, he exclaimed in surprise, "What's going on?"

The narrow road was almost blocked by emergency vehicles. Liz recognized a couple of Pleasant Creek cruisers, the sheriff's SUV, an ambulance, and a fire truck. A large tow truck with a winch was backed up to the water's edge.

Anxiety knotted Liz's belly. "I hope no one was hurt." She dreaded coming across automobile accidents and always breathed a prayer for those involved.

"I'm afraid he was."

Liz glanced at Jackson in surprise. His gaze was fixed on the vehicle slowly being retrieved from the water, men shouting guidance to the winch operator.

It appeared to be Horace Henry's black pickup.

11

Jackson pulled over to the side of the road. "Wait here, Liz." He jumped out of his car and trotted over to Chief Houghton, who stood watching the retrieval.

Liz closed her eyes, a wave of sickness rolling over her. Had Horace been in his truck when it went into the water? *How horrible.* Hugging herself, she sat frozen in her seat, praying and hoping that by some miracle he was all right.

By the dashboard clock, only ten minutes had passed when Jackson returned. "Liz? Are you okay?"

"I think so." Her voice was shaky. "What a shock." She could still feel the swooping jolt she'd experienced when she recognized the truck. "How bad is it?"

He slid into the seat and took her hand. "It's bad, I'm afraid. He was . . . inside when it went into the water."

"When did it happen? Can they tell?" Liz shuddered. Perhaps that was why the chief hadn't been able to get in touch with Horace.

"I'll spare you the details, but it may have happened the night we saw him out here. They'll have to do an examination, but they can tell it has been more than twenty-four hours."

"That's awful." Liz stared out the car window into the woods, not wanting to witness any of the activity taking place on the lake's shore. "How did they find him?"

"A fisherman caught his hook on the truck. The truck was in a deep pool, and if that hadn't happened, it might have been months before anyone found him."

Liz thought about the poor fisherman making such a gruesome discovery. "What now?"

"We'll get out of here in a minute, but the chief wants to ask you a few questions, if you don't mind."

"Of course not. Anything I can do to help."

At Jackson's signal, Houghton bustled over to the car. He stood on Jackson's side, the window open so they could talk. "So, Liz, Jackson said you saw Horace Henry out here the night you went to the Lakeside Inn."

"Yes, chief." She gave him the day and date. "I only met him once, at Jackson's factory that same evening. But he came to the inn while we were eating and then later, he almost ran us off the road. I recognized his truck." She pointed at the waterlogged vehicle. "That one."

Houghton paused in his note-taking. "Almost ran you off the road?"

"Didn't Jackson mention it? We were on our way back from dinner, at about ten o'clock or so, when Horace came at us in the wrong lane thankfully he swerved at the last minute."

The chief looked to Jackson for confirmation. "Is that what you recall happening?"

Jackson nodded. "Sure do. There was another car that came by right after, driving just as aggressively. I had to pull over for it too."

"Did you notice the make and model of the second vehicle?"

"It was dark," Liz said. "And it was going so fast. It was a four-door sedan, either black or navy. That's all I had time to notice." She thought of something. "Do you think whoever that was ran Horace off the road? This corner is after where we saw them, I think."

"It is," Jackson said. "Our incident happened farther back, a mile or two toward Pleasant Creek. The spot where there is a steep drop-off on the lake side of the road."

"We won't know for certain when Horace died—or how—until the medical examiner is done," Houghton said, tucking away his notebook. "But this is very helpful as far as establishing his movements, at least up to that night." He tapped the roof of the car. "Have a good evening."

Jackson reached to start the engine, then his hand dropped. "I hate to say it, Liz, but I don't really want to eat dinner at the Lakeside Inn anymore." He turned to face her. "I hate to disappoint you. I know you were looking forward to it."

Liz's appetite was gone too, so she was relieved at his suggested change in plans. "I don't care about going either, to be honest. Although I didn't know Horace, it's very upsetting." She put a hand on his arm. "I can't imagine how you feel. He *was* your employee."

Jackson stared out the windshield. "I just wonder if I could have prevented this somehow. I should have known by the erratic way he was acting that he was headed for disaster."

"It wasn't your fault, Jackson. It was an accident, a terrible tragedy." She thought for a minute. "How about this? Let's go back to the inn and I'll make us something light. We can relax in the four-season room and enjoy the sunset over Jaynes Lake."

"Sounds like a plan. Thanks for being understanding." He started the car and put it into gear, then backed up to turn and go the other way.

The ride back to town was far more somber than the journey out. Jackson was silent, almost morose, and Liz didn't want to disturb him. He was obviously attempting to deal with the unwelcome news that a man he'd known had died tragically.

Finally he broke the silence. "I regret that the last words I spoke to him were angry ones," he said. "I never had a chance to reconcile with him." His lips turned up in a brief smile. "Even if he did call the feds on me."

"That is hard," Liz said gently. She knew that Horace and Jackson might never have crossed paths again and had that opportunity. But there was always the possibility—as long as someone was alive. Now it was gone forever.

At the inn, Liz unlocked the door, noticing that none of her guests appeared to be in. Most of the time, guests went out to dinner, although they were welcome to bring food in and use the kitchen and dining room. Tonight she was glad to have the place to herself. Except for Beans, of course. He came trotting up to greet Jackson, tags jingling.

Jackson hunkered down to pat him. "You're a good old boy, aren't you?" Beans closed his eyes in bliss, tongue lolling.

Liz sent the dog a smile. Maybe he had sensed Jackson's distress, though she suspected that he actually just wanted the attention Jackson was always willing to give. "Why don't you two boys relax in the four-season room?" She thought quickly about the contents of her refrigerator. "Iced tea, cold fried chicken, and potato salad?"

Jackson raised his brows. "That sounds perfect. And here I thought I couldn't eat a bite." He nodded toward the kitchen. "Are you sure you don't want help?"

"Positive. Go ahead and I'll join you in a minute." In the kitchen, Liz tied a bib apron over her nice suit. She pulled a tray out of the cupboard and set two plates and silverware on it, followed by a platter of chicken, a bowl of potato salad, and glasses of tea. Salt and pepper shakers went into her pockets along with napkins.

Sunset skies over the small lake were clearly visible from the windowed wall of the four-season room. Jackson was seated on a rattan sofa, Beans on the floor beside him.

"Here already? You are fast."

"Being an innkeeper has honed my hostess skills." Liz set the tray on the table and emptied her pockets. "Help yourself." She went around the table and sat beside him on the long couch.

Jackson used the tongs to serve her a drumstick then put one on his own plate. Generous servings of potato salad studded with egg, green pepper, onion, and celery were next. He took a big, appreciative mouthful of salad then eyed the drumstick.

Liz laughed, reading his mind. "Go ahead and use your hands. It isn't fried chicken if you don't eat it that way."

He picked up the drumstick and took a big bite. "Yum. This *is* perfect."

Taking a daintier mouthful, Liz smiled to herself at the restorative power of a good meal. Although she had provided valuable services as an attorney, nothing beat helping people feel good, whether it was giving them a comfortable bed or a tasty meal. *Or*, she added mentally as Beans leaned against Jackson's leg, *the comfort only a loving dog can provide*.

Liz leaned back against the cushions, allowing herself to relax. The setting sun gilded a band of clouds pink and gold, the colors reflected in the still water of the tiny lake. A soft breeze came through the open screens, bringing the scents of fresh-cut grass and the flower beds that grew around the house foundation. Flowers inside, flowers outside—thanks to Kiera she was surrounded by the fragrant bounty of summer. Speaking of bounty . . .

"Remember I told you that animals have been raiding our vegetable garden?" Liz thought Jackson might appreciate the lighter topic. "They're still doing it. Poor Kiera is fit to be tied."

Jackson sat up a little straighter. "Really? What's doing it? Raccoons, deer, rabbits?"

"I'm not sure. I don't think she is either." Liz pointed to the garden situated on one side of the lawn. "She put a fence around it, but apparently the vegetables are still being eaten."

"That is a puzzle. Are they eating the whole vegetable or just parts of it?"

"Parts of them, mostly." Come to think of it, surely small animals would only nibble. Deer would probably gulp down the whole thing.

He raised his brows. "I have an idea. A camera. One of my buddies uses an infrared type to get photos of deer. Something like that would be perfect."

"It would be, since I think they only raid the garden at night."

"I'll ask him if we can borrow it for a few days. I'm sure he won't mind." Jackson picked up his iced tea and swirled it, making the cubes rattle, then drained it.

"Would you like a refill?" Liz asked.

"I'd love another glass of iced tea. You make the best." Jackson handed her the glass with a grin.

Liz rose from the sofa. "How about ice cream and berries for dessert?"

"I'll try to fit it in somewhere." He patted his midsection.

Smiling at his banter, Liz set the glass on the tray and carried the whole thing back to the kitchen. Here she unloaded the dirty plates, put away food, and dished up two small bowls of vanilla ice cream topped with fresh raspberries and a drizzle of chocolate syrup.

As they settled in with dessert, Liz said, "Three more days of the fair. Think they'll top today?" She was determined to keep the conversation on positive topics.

"I can't imagine how." Jackson's eyes were bright with excitement. "If that order comes through, I'll not only have that baseline of sales, but I'll also be able to be more efficient. The furniture store owner is going to focus on certain dining and bedroom sets, so I'll be able to buy wood in larger quantities. And the men can cut and stain pieces in bigger batches."

"So you'll make a larger profit?" Liz well knew the quest of the small business owner to fatten the bottom line—without compromising quality.

Jackson laughed. "I hope so. Then I can invest in more equipment and give my guys a well-deserved raise." He smiled. "And buy that sailboat."

A dog's snuffling and the click of claws were heard, then Rover trotted into the four-season room. He headed right to Beans and the two friends greeted each other.

"That one of your guests?" Jackson laughed, reaching out to scratch the hound's ears. "He's a sweetie."

"Actually, yes he is. His friend should be along any minute."

"Oops. Sorry to bother you, Liz. I was looking for Rover."

Liz gestured. "No problem. Come on in and meet our mayor, Jackson Cross." She smiled at Jackson. "He's also an amazing furniture maker."

"Quite a combo." John approached with his hand outstretched. "I'm John Smith. Nice to meet you, Jackson."

Jackson stood to shake hands, a frown creasing his brow. "Likewise. But you're not local? You look familiar."

John shrugged, his eyes on Rover and Beans, who lay side by side. "Maybe you saw me at the show today. Rover and I had quite a time strolling through the aisles. We must have circuited the place two or three times."

"Find anything good?" Liz asked. She was pleased her guest had taken her advice to attend the fair and seemed to have enjoyed it.

"I did. Some lovely wooden lamps. My sisters will be very pleased at Christmas this year."

"I got a head start on my shopping too," Liz said. She was racking her brain for something else to talk about without stepping into the minefield of the fair robberies when the sound of chattering was heard in the rotunda, fast approaching the kitchen. Brenda, Elaine, and Dolly were back.

"Let's forage for snacks!" one of the women shouted. "I'm still hungry after that tiny serving they gave me."

"Me too!" yelled the other. "I want a big fat sandwich."

A hunted expression crossed John's face and his head swiveled, seeking escape. "There isn't a back staircase in this place, is there?" He gave Jackson a weak smile. "Sometimes you just want to avoid company, you know what I mean?"

"I think Rover might enjoy a walk around the grounds," Liz said. "You can always circle back around and come in the front door."

"Good idea. We could both use a constitutional." With an effort, John got Rover to his feet and the duo slipped out the back door, followed by Beans, who wanted in on the action. And possibly also to avoid the women. They'd managed to actually tousle his very short fur that morning during an excess of petting. Beans loved affection as much as the next dog, but it seemed that he had his limits.

The moment the screen door slammed behind him, Brenda and Elaine rushed into the room, their vibrant presence like a force field. In the kitchen, water ran. Dolly must be doing something there.

The women spotted Jackson at the same moment, greetings to Liz dying on their lips. "Who are you?" Brenda asked. "I haven't seen *him* around here before." She shot Liz a resentful look as though accusing the innkeeper of hiding him in a closet.

"I'm not staying here," Jackson said. "I'm Jackson Cross, a friend of Liz's."

"A friend?" Brenda eyed Liz up and down in disbelief.

"Yes, I do have a few," Liz murmured, more amused than annoyed at her antics.

"We're Brenda Harris and Elaine Windsor," Brenda said. "From Sioux City."

"Nice to meet you both," Jackson said politely, his uneasy expression saying otherwise. He glanced at Liz, then cut his eyes to the back door, as though conveying that he understood John's hasty retreat.

Elaine studied the handsome mayor, cradling an elbow while tapping her lips. Recognition dawned. "I know. You make that sweet furniture. Remember, Brenda? But he was too busy to talk to us so we kept going."

Brenda perched on a nearby chair. "How did you do at the show today? Maybe we'll stop by tomorrow and take a look."

"I didn't know you sold furniture in your gift store," Liz said.

"We don't. But maybe we should." Brenda glanced over her shoulder. "What do you think, Elaine?"

"Maybe children's furniture. That's all we have room for." Elaine gave him a piercing look. "What's your pricing like? You're not going to gouge us, are you?"

Relief flowed over Jackson's features. "I don't make children's furniture. Only full-size pieces. Long, tall, heavy." He demonstrated with his hands.

Liz was thinking of suggesting a walk to Jackson when Dolly appeared in the doorway.

She put her hands on her tiny hips, a scowl on her pretty face. "Are y'all just gonna sit there and make me do all the work?"

"Dolly owns a toy shop," Liz whispered.

"That makes sense." Jackson appeared bemused at the sight of the diminutive shopkeeper with her high-piled blonde hair.

"Speaking of furniture, Dolly only buys really small pieces," Brenda said.

"Yes, for dollhouses," Elaine added, holding her forefinger and thumb two inches apart. "Think you could do that, Jackson?" She broke into laughter, joined by her friend.

Dolly's frown deepened. "I don't know what y'all are going on about, but I'm fixing to go to bed if you don't get in here and help." She turned to Liz. "I'm making sandwiches from the guest shelf, like you told us."

"Help yourself," Liz said. "Jackson and I were thinking of taking a turn around the lake, so we'll get out of your way." She forced a smile.

"Let's go," Dolly said to the others, sounding exactly like a scolding hen. "I don't know if you want mayo or mustard."

"Both," Brenda said, jumping up. "Pickles too, if she's got them."

"I do," Liz said. "Dill, bread-and-butter, and mustard pickle."

"My mouth's watering already," Elaine said. "Bring it on." As fast as they'd burst in, they exited.

"Wow," Jackson said, leaning back against the sofa. "If I wasn't exhausted before, I am now."

"There's never a dull moment around here," Liz said. "All my guests seem to be unique personalities. And honestly, I love that."

"I get it. It's the same thing with the mayor's job." He hoisted himself up out of the sofa, extending his hand out to Liz to help her up. "Let's go take our walk."

The first stars were beginning to twinkle, but as usual, in the summer at this hour, there was still enough light to stroll along the shore path. By unspoken mutual consent, Liz and Jackson were silent, focused on enjoying the sight of the sun sinking into the west and the lapping lake water.

They were almost completely around when another figure appeared in the dusk, tall and male, striding with purpose. Involuntarily, Liz clutched Jackson's arm, her quickly aroused fear revealing the barely contained anxiety she had been suppressing.

As he drew closer, Liz noticed he wore a cowboy hat. When he spotted them, he took it off and inclined his head in a nod. "Howdy, Liz. Jackson." With a release of tension, Liz recognized Tommy Dunn.

"Are you taking a stroll?" Liz asked. "It's a great night for it."

Tommy sighed. "Not exactly. I came looking for you." He shuffled his feet in their pointed boots. "I'm not who I said I was, Miss Liz, sorry to say. My business here has nothing to do with the fair." He swallowed. "I'm a bounty hunter, and I just learned my target is dead."

12

Liz gaped at him. "Want to say that again?" Her mind reeled as she tried to assimilate this new information. Her guest was a bounty hunter? She'd never met one in person, having only read about them in books or seen them on television.

Before Tommy could answer, Jackson said, "Why don't we go back to the house. I think I need to sit down." He sent Tommy a sidelong glance. "That is, if you're talking about my ex-employee."

"Yes, sir, I am." Tommy settled his hat more firmly on his head and turned on his heel, leading the way toward the inn.

Afraid they might be interrupted by the other guests, Liz suggested they go to her quarters. Here she settled the two tall men in her sitting room, which seemed even smaller with their presence. She went to the kitchenette. "Anyone want ice water?"

The others assented, silent until she served tall glasses. Liz perched on a rocking armchair. "All right, Tommy. Want to take it from the top?"

The Texan rubbed his chin with two fingers. "Once again, I apologize for the deception, Liz. But I couldn't risk the truth of my purpose here being known."

Liz rocked in the chair, taking a welcome sip of cold water. "Don't worry about it. I don't expect my guests to share their personal business."

Tommy sighed and shook his head. "I'm still wrapping my head around the fact that Horace Henry Clegg is dead—"

Jackson interrupted. "Did you say Horace Henry *Clegg*?" He fidgeted on the sofa. "That means he was working for me under a false name."

"That's right, his last name is, er, *was* Clegg. Says so right on his birth certificate."

Liz put two and two together. "And the house he was staying in belonged to a Clegg. The one that burned?"

Tommy whistled. "You are one sharp filly. That place belonged to Horace's great-uncle. He passed away last year. It was that tenuous connection that brought me here, on his trail."

Jackson leaned forward in his seat. "But why were you chasing him? What did he do?"

Tommy's narrow eyes shifted back and forth as he studied Liz and Jackson in turn. Finally, he sighed. "What I tell you can't leave this room. If you mention it to anyone, you'll be putting yourselves in danger. Is that clear?"

Unease iced Liz's core. What kind of trouble had Jackson's employee brought to Pleasant Creek?

"Crystal clear," Jackson said. "Tell us."

"Horace stole a significant sum of money from a very bad man." After glancing around, he lowered his voice to a gravelly rumble. "The kind of man who puts out hits on people."

Liz and Jackson absorbed this unwelcome news in silence for a long moment. Then Jackson broke the quiet with a bark of disbelieving laughter. "Seriously? Horace on the run from a crime boss?" He made a display of glancing around. "Are you from one of those reality television shows or something?"

I hope this is a prank. Otherwise Jackson could be in danger. What if the crime boss thought he was responsible for harboring Horace? Liz firmly shut off the direction of her thoughts. *Don't jump to conclusions.*

"I thought you might react that way. Hey, I might have myself if I didn't know better." He pointed at Liz's laptop, sitting on the desk. "Can I hop on the Internet for a minute?"

"Help yourself." Liz went to the computer and turned it on, then logged in. "Here you go."

Tommy settled himself at the desk, dwarfing it and the laptop, while Liz put together a plate of cookies from her personal stash. She needed something to do with her hands. Jackson took one off the plate, chewing it absently. "I'm still having trouble getting my head around this," he confided.

"Me too." Liz refrained from eating a cookie. Her throat was too dry, despite drinking a glass of water.

"All right, take a look at this." Tommy pushed back so the other two could see the headline on the screen: *Alleged Leader of Crime Ring Behind Bars.* The site was a Houston television station, and the page was dated several months prior.

They watched a video detailing the arrest and pending trial of a man who was said to have operated a money-laundering ring throughout Texas.

"How does Horace fit in?" James asked.

"He was supposed to testify against his former boss, but instead he went on the run. With a bag full of money."

"And came here. So who are you working for?" Jackson eyed the bounty hunter with suspicion.

"Am I a white hat or a black hat, you mean?" Tommy laughed. "I work for myself. The feds wanted Horace, and I wanted the huge reward. It was a mutually beneficial business arrangement." He edged Jackson aside and brought a wanted poster up on the screen. "And yes, I'm licensed. And insured." He pulled out his wallet and displayed the paperwork.

Jackson studied the cards then passed the wallet to Liz. They appeared legitimate. Then Jackson said what she was thinking. "Horace was a fugitive from the law. And now he's dead."

Was Horace's death an accident or something more sinister? And where is the money he supposedly stole?

"This is all very fascinating, Tommy," Jackson said. "But why are you telling us? Liz and I don't know anything."

Tommy sucked air through his teeth. "To be honest, I need your help. I want to retrace Horace's steps here in Pleasant Creek, and it seemed to me, as his employer, you might have some idea where he hung out and who his associates were."

"Do you think he was murdered?" Liz asked. Maybe Tommy was going to investigate.

"It's not for me to say. But whatever happened—"

"The money is still missing and you want to find it." Jackson's tone was triumphant. "That's it, isn't it? You still want the reward. Or at least part of it."

Tommy's big feet shuffled on the carpet. "Yes, I do. I can still get paid if I return what he stole. I've got a lot invested in this case. I'd even be willing to split it." He leaned closer. "Besides, Horace might have had some evidence with him, something that could put away his boss—crime boss, that is—for good."

"You really think so?" Jackson's brow knit in concern. "Finding that is pretty important then."

As though sensing a softening, Tommy's posture relaxed. "Then you'll help me?"

"Maybe." Jackson held up a hand. "But whatever I tell you, I'm also going to share with the police."

"Fair enough. As long as someone gets to the bottom of this, that's what counts, right?" Tommy leaned forward, clasping his hands between his knees. "I already know his last address. So the next thing I need is his employment record to see what that tells us."

Jackson shook his head. "Sorry. That would be breaking the law. I can't do that."

Tommy accepted that with a shrug. "I understand. But if you could see your way to telling me anything you remember, that would be much appreciated." Tommy rose from the chair. "It's getting late so I'll leave you be." At the door, he halted, hand on the knob. "Be careful, both of you. Forget I ever spoke to you about any of this, okay?" He pointed at Liz. "As far as you're concerned, I'm still a buyer from Houston, Texas, here for the fair. I don't want a nice lady like you mixed up in this nasty business." With a rattle of the door, he was gone.

His absence felt like the calm after a huge storm. Liz and Jackson sat in silence for a long moment. Finally, Jackson spoke. "Wow. Just . . . wow." He shook his head. "I thought Horace was difficult and even a troublemaker. But to find out he was involved with a crime ring? And your guest is a bounty hunter on his trail?"

"I'm as stunned as you are." Liz tried to take in a deep breath but her chest was tight with dread. Tommy had been dead serious when he'd issued that warning. "And I'm scared. What if—Jackson, they might come after you."

"I'm not worried about me," Jackson said. "I can take care of myself. But please, Liz, be careful," He glanced around. "Keep your doors and windows locked, and don't go out alone at night."

Now that Jackson was expressing concern for *her* safety, Liz felt compelled to reassure him. After all, what did she know about Horace Henry? She'd never even officially met the man. She said as much. "I'll do that. Plus I've got Tommy staying here. He's on the alert, as he said." *And now his remark about securing the perimeter makes sense.*

Jackson grunted. "Still, keep your eyes open, okay? Dunn's not going to be with you constantly."

"I will," Liz promised. "Another thing. Where do you suppose Horace's money is? If the police found it in the car, they haven't said."

"I'm sure Tommy would know if they had. He'd be back in Texas already. There'd be no reason to stay here."

"True. I hope it wasn't in the house that burned."

"And that's another thing. Why did someone burn the house down? Too strange." Jackson rose to his feet with a groan. "This has been nice, but I guess I should head home. Big day tomorrow."

Liz got up too. "I'll walk you out."

"I'm sorry about dinner," he said as they crossed the rotunda. "Rain check?"

"Absolutely. Why don't we wait until after the fair? Things are crazy while the fair is going on."

"And with the death of my employee, apparently." Jackson gave a rueful laugh. He nodded toward the sitting room, where the other guests were excitedly discussing the latest news.

"I heard the dead guy worked for that furniture maker," Brenda said. Elaine shrieked in response.

"That's my cue. Good night, Liz." Jackson slipped out the front door with a wave.

"Good night, Jackson." Liz shut the front door. Could she escape back to her quarters or should she do the right thing and check on her guests? With a sigh and a sense she was putting on a breastplate of armor, she did her duty as innkeeper. She went into the sitting room.

"Liz! Are we glad to see you. We heard you were there when . . ."

───── *ⵊⵊⵊⵊⵊⵊⵊⵊⵊⵊⵊⵊⵊⵊⵊⵊ* ─────

Bad news sure does travel fast. Horace Henry Clegg's scowl, no doubt lifted from his driver's license, met Liz's gaze from the front page of the *Fort Wayne Times* the next morning. She plopped the paper on the table then went to the stove to rescue her pot of oatmeal. A splash of cream, fresh raspberries, and a drizzle of honey completed the dish.

Texas Man's Death in Accident Investigated, read the headline. Only the bare details were given—the discovery of the truck by fishermen and the attempts to determine cause of death. "Parties of interest will be questioned," Chief Houghton was quoted as saying. *What does that mean?* Worse, an enterprising reporter had discovered that Horace had worked at Cross Furniture and had recently been fired. Also mentioned was the house burning down at the old Clegg farm. No wonder the regional paper had covered the incident. It read like a plot from an action movie.

The oatmeal turned to paste in her mouth but Liz forced herself to finish. The guests were due for breakfast any minute and she needed to keep her strength up for an active day.

She was preparing soft-boiled eggs when her cell phone rang. It was Sadie. "Did you see the *Times*?" was Sadie's greeting. "I spit out my coffee all over the table when I saw that one of Jackson's former employees was dead."

"Tell me about it. We were there when they retrieved the truck." Liz checked the timer. Too long and the eggs would be hard-boiled, not as much fun to eat with toast.

"What?" Sadie's voice rose to a squawk. "That's horrible. How did that happen?"

Liz took her friend through the sequence of events the previous evening, omitting Tommy's revelations about Horace's connection to a crime ring. The fewer people dragged into a dangerous situation the better.

"Do you think the car accident and the fire were related?" Sadie asked. "No one could have that much bad luck."

Liz sighed. *Trust Sadie to connect the dots.* "I don't know, but probably. What are the chances otherwise?"

"Well, be careful then. And tell Jackson to watch out. It looks like that employee was mixed up in something pretty bad." Sadie sighed. "I'm getting ready to head out to the fair. Hopefully the security team will have some answers for us. They were supposed to review the video footage."

"I hope they catch whoever it is. Let me know if you need me, okay?"

"Will do. Opal is planning on coming for the day, so we should be all right. Thanks for offering." Sadie hung up.

Liz pulled the eggs off the stove and picked up a slotted spoon to remove them from the water. Then she filled the toaster with bread slices and put the oatmeal in a tureen.

Her phone rang again, making her jump. Without looking, she snatched it up. "Hello. This is Liz." She propped it between her shoulder and ear, trying to keep breakfast preparations going.

"Ms. Eckardt? This is the dispatcher at the Pleasant Creek Police Station. The chief would like you to come down for questioning about Mr. Clegg."

A feeling of foreboding swept over Liz as she agreed to go down in an hour or so. She had the sneaking suspicion that Horace's death might not be an accident after all.

"Good morning," Brenda's voice was gratingly loud and cheerful when Liz entered the dining room. She took in Liz from head to toe. "What's wrong? You look like you lost your best friend."

Liz made a brushing-off gesture. "Sorry. Just woolgathering." She busied herself with the serving dishes.

"Let me help you." Her guest picked up the blue bowl of eggs, carrying it gingerly toward the dining room while Liz brought a platter of toast.

"Did you hear about that man they found in the lake?" Brenda shuddered in delight. "How awful."

"I did hear something about that, yes. So tragic." Liz set the platter down. "I need to get the oatmeal and fixings, and then we're ready."

Brenda followed her back to the kitchen. "I can't imagine being a police officer or an emergency medical professional. Can you imagine how gruesome that body must have looked after being in the lake?" She lowered her voice to a whisper. "Do you suppose fish nibbled on him?"

Liz recoiled. "Please, I just ate."

Unrepentant, the woman burst into laughter. "You sound like Elaine. She has a weak stomach too."

Somehow Liz made it through the rest of the preparations, ferrying coffee, juice, and a pot of tea to the table along with the food. Once the other guests descended—save for Tommy who must have left earlier—she was able to avoid being drawn into the conversation about Horace. John didn't join in, but the three women chewed over the subject with great pleasure. Once they were finally quiet for a moment, having apparently exhausted the topic, Liz judged it safe to go back in with a coffee refill.

"I heard your friends got robbed," Elaine said to Liz, who nearly spilled her coffee in surprise at this statement.

Here we go again. What wouldn't Liz give for guests who minded their own business.

Dolly tut-tutted. "Those nice ladies with the quilts? That's awful."

"Yes, the Sew Welcome booth," Brenda said. "We bought some things from them." She turned to Liz. "So what have you heard?"

"I really can't discuss it," Liz said. "It's in the hands of the police and the security team."

"Security team." Brenda scoffed. "They're your typical small-town amateurs."

"That's why I always carry my money and cards right here." Dolly patted her upper chest. "I'd notice if someone tried to rob me."

"I'm thinking of putting my money in my shoe," Elaine said. "That way no one can get anything important if they pick my pocket or steal my wallet out of my purse." She flapped her blouse. "Anything I put up here would slide right through."

John stifled a laugh, covering it up by pretending to sneeze. His eyes were bright with merriment over the napkin he held to his face. Liz bit her lip, managing to suppress her laughter until she got back into the kitchen.

Beans looked up at her with wary eyes, causing her to laugh again. "I'm sorry, Beans, but it's all too much right now." She bent to fondle his head. "I have to go be questioned by the police."

Sarah arrived as Liz was taking off her apron, the interminable meal finally over. "I'm so glad you're here. I have to run out for an appointment." Liz was usually pretty open with the young Amish woman, but today she didn't even want to mention that she was headed to the police station. To do so might unleash the anxiety humming in her veins as the appointment grew closer.

"That's fine. I'll do the dishes and make up the rooms. Today we need to change the sheets, right? I'll run a couple of loads of wash too." She peered outside at the blue sky and sunshine. "Maybe I can hang the laundry outside. It always smells so fresh when we do that."

"I don't know what I'd do without you, Sarah." Liz's words were heartfelt. She ran a brush through her hair, grabbed her purse, and headed out, eager to get the ordeal over with. She hadn't felt this way since going in for medical tests required to "take a closer look," as the doctor put it. That situation had turned out favorably, and she hoped this one would too.

Ten minutes later, she arrived at the Pleasant Creek police station. It was a nondescript brick building downtown, placed off Main Street. Liz found a spot nearby to park and quickly headed inside, her heart thumping. *What's wrong with you?* she scolded herself. *It's not like this is your first time here.* But she was unable to shake the uneasy sense of foreboding that followed her like a shadow.

As she reached for the handle of the glass door, she heard footsteps coming along the sidewalk from the other direction. Turning to look, she spotted Jackson, who gave her a wave.

"They called you down here too?" He reached out and opened the door for her. "Well, let's hurry up and get this foolishness over with."

Liz hesitated on the threshold. "What's going on? Do you know?"

Jackson lifted one shoulder. "Somehow they got the boneheaded idea that I killed Horace Henry."

13

Liz froze. "Are you saying Horace was *murdered* and they think *you* did it?" She flushed hot then cold, a wave of sickness rolling in her belly and sending liquid up into her throat. She quickly swallowed, hoping she wouldn't lose her breakfast right there in public, on the steps.

Jackson made a shooing motion, indicating she should go in. "That's exactly what I'm saying. Come on, let's go in." He lowered his voice to a whisper. "They won't be happy if they see us talking. They'll think we're in cahoots." He smiled to let her know he was joking.

Obviously Jackson thought the whole thing was only a misunderstanding and would soon blow over. Trying to feel reassured, Liz stepped inside, forcing her numb legs to move. Jackson followed.

The dispatcher sat behind a window, a young woman who looked barely old enough to drive, but was probably in her twenties. "May I help you?"

"We're here to see the chief," Liz said. "Liz Eckardt and Jackson Cross."

"Have a seat and I'll tell him you're here." She picked up the telephone.

They moved to the row of plastic chairs in the narrow hallway and settled down, a couple of chairs apart. Liz was dying to ask Jackson for details, but she couldn't under the officer's watchful and curious eye. She glanced over. He was leaning back in the chair, one ankle resting on the other knee, hands behind his head, staring at the ceiling as if he didn't have a care in the world. He really wasn't worried, she realized. The knot in her belly loosened slightly.

"Liz?" Chief Houghton stood in the doorway to the right, a

stern expression on his face. His eyes flicked past Liz to Jackson, and he frowned. "Come on in."

Liz jumped to her feet, feeling as guilty as if she had been fraternizing with a criminal. Had the chief already tried and condemned Jackson in his mind? That wasn't like the man known for his evenhanded approach to investigations.

The chief led her into a small interview room containing only a table, several chairs, and a video monitor attached to the wall. "Have a seat. We're going to record the interview, with your permission."

"That's fine." Liz sat at the table, wincing at the hard discomfort of the chair. Between this one and the waiting room, her behind was going to be sore. "Can you tell me what's going on?" She wanted to blurt out the ridiculous news that Jackson thought he was a suspect, but she managed to bite back the words.

"All in good time." Houghton settled at the table, starting with establishing remarks as to day, date, and time, and interview subject Elizabeth Eckardt.

Liz gave her age and address, then waited with held breath for the questions to begin. Maybe she could glean information indirectly, based on the questions.

"Where were you on . . . ?" The chief asked her movements the day she and Jackson had gone to the Lakeside Inn.

"So you went to Cross Furniture to meet Jackson? Take me through what happened there."

Liz described her arrival at the factory, the raised voices she heard, and Horace Henry Clegg's abrupt departure.

"What did Jackson say after Horace left?"

"I don't remember exactly, but he didn't seem angry or especially upset. It was like he was disappointed in how things turned out with Horace. He told me as much during dinner."

Houghton put up a hand. "One thing at a time. What happened after Horace left the factory?"

Liz described how Jackson had driven them to the inn, where Alfred Clegg greeted them. Alfred *Clegg*. Her words faltered.

Houghton's tone was sharp. "Did you remember something?"

"No . . . it just clicked that Alfred and Horace have the same last name."

"Go on. What happened during dinner?"

"Not much—except Horace showed up and was talking to Alfred in the hallway outside the dining room." Liz leaned forward in her seat. "Don't you see, he was there to visit Alfred. Jackson, of course, thought he'd followed us, so he went out to talk to him. But Horace had left Cross Furniture before we did, so how could he have ended up behind us? I didn't see him on the way out there."

"Perhaps he knew Jackson's plans in advance. They weren't secret, were they?"

"You'll have to ask Jackson that." Liz was miffed. Did the chief have blinders on? "At least talk to Alfred. Maybe he wasn't too happy to have a criminal relative on the grounds." She winced as her words echoed in her own ears. Tommy had spoken to them in confidence.

Of course the chief jumped right on her blunder. "What do you mean, criminal?"

Liz ducked her head, studying her interlaced hands. "I heard Horace was on the run." She forced herself to make eye contact. "But don't ask me how I know." *Can he make me?*

To her relief, Houghton merely grunted. "I have a pretty good idea where you heard that already. But Horace's background—and family—aren't the focus here. What time did you and Jackson leave the inn?"

"I think it was about ten or so." Liz racked her brain for the timeline, explaining that they'd taken a walk along the shore before leaving. She sat up straight as she remembered the incident on the lake road. "Horace almost ran us over on the way back to town."

"You mentioned that when we were retrieving his truck. What happened?" At Houghton's spark of interest, Liz realized with a sinking stomach that she might not have helped Jackson's case.

She reluctantly relayed what had happened. "But that's not all," she said. "There was another car chasing Horace. He almost ran us over too."

"He? Did you see the driver?"

She reviewed the memory in her mind. Had she seen the passengers in the sedan? "I'm afraid not. It was dark. It was only because I had seen Horace's truck earlier that I recognized him. But I did notice the other vehicle was a four-door sedan."

Houghton made a note but didn't seem impressed. "People drive fast on that road a lot. Hard to tell if the two incidents were related."

The chief was right of course. But Liz couldn't shake the idea that his thoughts were aimed firmly in one direction—toward Jackson's guilt.

When she was released a while later, there wasn't any sign of Jackson in the waiting area. "Did Jackson Cross leave already?" she asked the dispatcher.

She shook her head. "Mr. Cross is still here. Is there anything else I can help you with?"

Liz hesitated. She'd have to catch up with Jackson later. "No thanks. Have a good day."

Outside the day was still sunny and cheerful, a light breeze ruffling the green leaves on the trees around the town square. But to Liz, everything felt dark. She thought of Jackson in an interrogation room, facing accusations of murder. But he was innocent, so surely it would all be cleared up quickly.

Back at the inn, Sarah had finished the rooms. "The guests are all out," she reported. "I think they're at the fair. Are you going over?"

"Maybe I will." Then she remembered. "I meant to tell you. Have you heard about Wendy Felder, the woman who was homeless? I hired her to help us clean my quarters this afternoon. Remember that spring cleaning we meant to give it?" They had been so busy that the project had been put on hold in favor of concentrating on the inn.

"That is so nice. I'm sure she appreciates the work."

"She seemed to. And if she does a good job we can give her a recommendation." Liz glanced at the clock. Noon. She wasn't really hungry, but she supposed she needed to keep her strength up. "Let's have lunch."

Soon after they finished eating salads topped with cheese and diced ham in the four-season room, the doorbell rang. "That must be Wendy," Liz said.

"I'll clear up while you get her started," Sarah said. "Then I'll come help."

Wendy was indeed at the door, along with her husband and son. Earl Felder was a tall man with a drooping mustache and kind eyes.

"Good afternoon, Liz." Wendy introduced Liz to her family. "Earl and Austin thought they'd take a walk around the lake before heading back to the motel. Then they'll come back and get me."

"They don't have to do that," Liz said. "You two can hang out here if you want. I've got a big yard and some balls and other toys." She maintained a trunk of outdoor sporting goods for her more active guests and those with children.

"Thank you," Earl said. He turned to his son. "Doesn't that sound great, Austin?"

Austin nodded. "Thank you, Ms. Eckardt." He spotted Kiera trudging across the lawn carrying gardening tools. "What is she doing?"

"Kiera's my gardener," Liz said. "This afternoon she's working on the vegetable garden."

Austin looked up at his dad. "Can I help?"

Earl glanced at Liz, who nodded. "Sure, if Kiera wants your help. We'll ask her."

The boy smiled. "I love to garden."

Wendy ruffled her son's hair. "That's news to me, but have fun."

After spending a couple of hours working with Wendy and Sarah to deep-clean her bathroom, kitchenette, and windows, Liz headed over to the fair. A good number of cars were in the parking lot. *Good. That means interest is still there.* Inside, she swung past Jackson's booth on her way to Sew Welcome's, just in case Jackson was there. Curtis, his employee, was by himself. "Liz," he called. "Have you seen Jackson?"

"I was going to ask you the same thing." Liz decided not to mention seeing his boss at the police station. "Did he tell you when he'd be here?"

Curtis frowned, looking at his phone and scrolling through messages. "He texted me this morning and said he was delayed but would be in touch. I haven't heard from him since."

"I'm sure you will," Liz said. "I know he's excited about being here. And he wouldn't leave you in the lurch." She bit her lip. Jackson must still be tied up at the police station—otherwise he would have communicated with Curtis. What could be going on?

Screaming from a nearby booth labeled Berta's Baskets caught their attention. "I've been robbed!" a middle-aged woman cried. She ran both hands through her curly gray hair, distraught. On the table in front of her, a cashbox hung open. "Someone took all my money!"

The news rippled through the crowd, and people surged toward the booth, curious and concerned. Liz managed to sidle through by turning sideways and insistently forging a path, murmuring, "Excuse me" and "I'm sorry."

When she reached the distraught woman, she smiled reassuringly. "Hi, I'm Liz Eckardt. The same thing happened to my friends." Liz pulled out her phone. "Did you call the police or security?"

"Not yet." The woman rubbed a shaking hand across her wet eyes. "I'm still in shock, I guess."

Realizing the police were probably tied up with Horace's murder, Liz called security. She reached Ronnie, the head officer. "Not again," he said with a groan after Liz explained the situation. "We told people not to use cashboxes. I'll send someone over right away. And I'll call the police."

Liz returned to the woman in the booth. "They'll be right here," Liz said.

"Thanks." She paced about, straightening the gorgeous baskets filling her booth. Made for every purpose, they ranged from tiny round containers to enormous laundry baskets.

Liz admired a pie basket with a wooden lid. "What beautiful work. Are you Berta?"

"I am." Berta smiled shyly as she continued to rearrange her stock.

A familiar ponytail bobbed through the crowd, which parted to allow Darlene from the security office through. She rested both hands on her hips, legs in a wide stance. "What's this about a robbery?"

Berta showed her the empty cashbox. "This had several hundred dollars in it."

Darlene peered into the empty box. "You didn't happen to see who took it, did you?"

"No, I honestly don't have a clue. It's like it vanished into thin air."

Darlene took a good look at Liz. "Haven't I seen you somewhere before?"

"Yes. My friends at the Sew Welcome booth were also robbed."

"So you were there." Darlene pointed. "And here. Hmm. What a coincidence."

Liz took a step back, her mouth opening with shock. "Hold on," she said once she got her face muscles to cooperate. "I had nothing to do with the robberies."

"You have to admit it's odd." Darlene turned to Berta. "Did you wait on this woman?"

"I . . . I don't think so." Berta put both hands to her head. "But I'm not sure of anything right now."

Great. Just great. Liz sighed with exasperation. "I came over when I heard you screaming. And I'm the one who called security."

Darlene had the nerve to wink. "Good way to cover your tracks."

The temptation to throttle the obnoxious security guard was growing, but fortunately Liz remembered something. She dug into her pocket and pulled out her entry ticket. "Look at the time stamp on this. You'll see I barely had enough time to get in here, let alone rob someone. My first and only stop was at Cross Furniture. You can ask Curtis."

The guard reluctantly took the ticket and studied it with pursed lips, even turning it over as if it might be a fake. She handed it back with a shrug. "No need to take offense. Just doing my job."

And not very well. At least three vendors have been robbed. But Liz knew it wouldn't pay to confront the woman. "Now that you're here, I'll leave matters in your capable hands." She hoped Darlene didn't pick up on the sarcasm that crept into her voice. "Good luck, Berta. I hope they find whoever did this and you get your money back."

Berta gave her a tearful smile. "I'm sure it's long gone, but I appreciate the thought. Thanks for your help."

"No problem." With a nod, Liz slipped from behind the booth

and made her way through the tightly packed throng. The sight of the Sew Welcome booth beckoned and she hurried over, eager to see her friends. What a day she'd had, being questioned by the police *and* suspected of stealing.

Opal looked up from folding a quilt as Liz drew near. "Liz, thank goodness." Her serious expression belied her pleasant words and Liz felt a tinge of foreboding.

"What's going on? Is everything all right?" Sadie and Mary Ann were both waiting on customers at the other end of the booth. They looked to be in one piece.

"We're fine," Opal said. "But I can't say the same about Jackson." She leaned closer and whispered, "They arrested him for murder."

14

Liz swayed on her feet, scarcely able to believe her ears. "When did this happen?"

"Let's get you to a seat." Opal came around and grabbed Liz's arm, guiding her to a chair at the back of the enclosure. "In answer to your question, it happened just now." She handed Liz Mary Ann's phone and pressed a button. "Watch."

A news reporter stood in front of the Pleasant Creek police department. "The mayor of the idyllic small farming community of Pleasant Creek was arrested today for murder. This man"—they flashed a picture of Horace—"was found late last night in his vehicle, submerged in Crystal Lake. However, his tragic death wasn't an accident."

Chief Houghton came on the screen, obviously upset but doing his best to remain professional. "Jackson Cross was first questioned as a person of interest, but we've found enough evidence to press charges . . ."

Liz exited the video, too nauseated to listen to more. "What evidence? That's ludicrous."

"That's what we think," Opal said, "so we're holding an emergency meeting of the Material Girls tonight." Her lips quirked in grim humor. "With one Material Man. Jackson will be there."

"He's not in jail?" Liz had pictured him languishing behind bars, probably already dressed in an orange jumpsuit.

"His crackerjack attorney got him out on bail already. Nina Davis, from Blaketown." Blaketown was a nearby city.

Liz immediately felt better. "She is good. She cleared Mary Ann's name with no trouble over that pie incident a while back, remember?" She slumped back in the folding cloth chair, momentarily overcome by the news. "We've got to help him. I know he's innocent."

"Hold that thought," Opal said as a trio of middle-aged shoppers bustled up to the booth. "We need to make hay while the sun shines. Want to help?"

Rallying, Liz jumped up and joined Opal at the counter. For a couple of hours, she threw herself into discussing quilt patterns, helping customers pick their favorites from an array of beautiful fabrics, and taking down contact information for mailing lists. Mary Ann and Sadie were working equally hard, and the troubled glances they sent Liz communicated their own distress over their beloved mayor and friend.

Late in the afternoon, Curtis came by the booth. Despite his youth, he was drawn and gray with fatigue, a frown creasing his brow. "I heard what happened, Liz. I worked the booth on my own."

"How did it go? Get a lot of sales?"

"Worse than none. The Chicago buyer came by and canceled." He blinked rapidly and Liz had the feeling he was holding back tears. "How am I going to tell Jackson?"

"He won't blame you," Liz said. "Besides, he's got bigger problems than a lost order right now." *Like possibly spending the rest of his life in jail. What evidence could the police possibly have found?*

As Curtis departed, Darlene swaggered up to the booth, greeting Liz with a nod. "Can I speak to the owners?" she asked Liz.

"Of course." Liz called for Mary Ann, who was closest, to come over.

"Do you have news for us?" Mary Ann was eager. "I hope you found our money."

Darlene put up a hand. "Not so fast." She chewed gum vigorously for a minute. "But we may have a lead. That's all. Wanted you to know." With another nod, she hitched her belt and walked off.

"I think that job is going to her head," Mary Ann whispered. "She acts stranger every time I see her."

"She must be watching too many cop movies." Liz watched as the guard stopped to guffaw with a fellow employee. "But, hopefully, they'll solve these thefts."

━━━━━ /////////////////////////// ━━━━━

"Come on in." Liz stood back to let Jackson enter the inn. "Everyone is here."

He stepped inside the foyer, glancing back over his shoulder. "I think I managed to dodge the press. I had to do some evasive driving on the way over."

Liz looked outside but the street appeared quiet in the summer twilight, the only sounds sleepy birds and crickets. "I can't believe they're chasing you."

Jackson ran his hand through his hair and grimaced. "I'm big news. It's already hit the tabloids. 'Small-Town Mayor—Big-Time Criminal?' was one headline. They're trying to tie me to Horace's activities in Houston."

"That's horrible." Liz despised the way the media sometimes seized a story, often condemning people without a trial, despite the use of "allegedly" as a disclaimer.

"I'm trying to keep my focus where it needs to be, on proving my innocence."

Footsteps thudded upstairs, announcing the presence of guests. Liz put a finger to her lips. "Let's continue this discussion in the store."

She rapped on the glass door and Mary Ann came to let them in. "Jackson. So glad you made it." She gave the mayor a warm hug. "We're behind you all the way."

The other women—Sadie, Opal, Naomi, and Caitlyn—greeted

him warmly also. "With you on my side, how can I lose?" Jackson's voice was husky with gratitude.

They settled him at one of the long tables with a cup of coffee, then picked up their stitching. "We're making quilted place mats and a child's quilt for one of our families," Naomi said. "Wendy and Earl and their little boy, Austin. The Borkholder family donated a queen-size wedding-ring quilt, by the way. It's gorgeous." She displayed a picture on her phone.

After the oohs and ahhs died down, Liz said, "So it's official? They got the apartment?" She placed several colorful squares together to test her design. Austin was getting a quilt made of fabric that featured cars, trains, and boats.

"They sure did. We're having furniture delivered in a day or two so they can move in next week."

"Don't forget the dining set Jackson donated," Liz said. "It's a beauty."

"Happy to do it," Jackson said. His phone dinged. He glanced at the message and groaned.

"More reporters?" Liz asked.

"No. It's from the fair organizers. 'Under the circumstances,' they want me to pull out. And you know I lost the Chicago buyer. That was a blow."

"Nothing like kicking a man when he's down." Sadie's blue eyes flashed with anger. "Whatever happened to innocent until proven guilty?"

"I can't blame them. The press will probably clog the place if I go back."

They worked in silence for a few minutes, the strains of soothing classical music playing in the background from the music system. Finally, Liz broke the ice. She had to know. "Jackson, why did they arrest you? You weren't anywhere near the lake when Horace drowned."

Jackson twirled his coffee cup in his hands. "Actually, Liz, I did go back out there that night, after I dropped you off."

Liz fumbled her squares of cloth. "Really? Why?" She held her breath waiting for his answer.

"I realized when I got home that I'd left my credit card at the restaurant. So I drove back out to get it. I could have waited, but with the fair and all, it would have been days before I could go out there again."

"So you were out at the lake. Big deal." Sadie's tone was no nonsense. "It's a stretch from that minor incident to say you killed someone."

Jackson's mouth twisted. "But you see, Horace didn't drown. He was killed by a blow to the head. With a table leg from my factory."

"How do they know that?" Caitlyn asked.

"It was in the car. Apparently they can get fingerprints off wet wood. And one of mine was on it. They're considering the fact that Horace called OSHA on me to be motive. They think I ran into him out at the lake, we argued, and I killed him, then hid his body, truck and all." He turned to Liz. "Remember my offhand remark about 'Horace's legacy' when those agents turned up? The chief is convinced I knew Horace was dead."

"Chief Houghton is going along with this?" Sadie pressed her lips together. "I thought you two were friends."

"We are, have been for years. And this is tearing him up, I can tell. But he's got to go along with the prosecutor. He's the one who brought charges against me."

Opal gasped. "This whole thing is horrible."

Liz agreed. Not only was it a terrible way to die, the killer must have deliberately tried to frame Jackson. Unless . . . "You don't think someone else from the factory killed him, do you?"

"Gosh, I hate to think that." Jackson thought for a minute. "And

I can't think of who would have done it. The men didn't like Horace, but no one hated him. They're all good men."

"That you know of," Sadie said. "This is the ugly part of investigations. You have to look at everyone." She nodded at Jackson. "But that's not the same as considering them guilty."

"Get this," Liz said. "Horace had relatives around here. He was living in his great-uncle's house. Remember the house fire? That's the place."

Caitlyn whistled. "Maybe his murder has nothing to do with Jackson's company."

Liz glanced at Jackson, who seemed to read her mind. "Wait. There's more." She took a deep breath, realizing she was about to break Tommy's confidence. But these were her friends. If she could trust anyone in the world, it was these ladies. "Horace was on the run from a gang in Houston. He was due to testify, but he came to Indiana instead."

Mary Ann nodded thoughtfully. "So maybe trouble followed him here."

"The question is, how did they get hold of that table leg?" Opal asked. "That worries me."

"It was part of the sample sets we use," Jackson said. "Each one has half a dozen legs to exhibit different kinds of wood and styles."

"I remember seeing those sample legs at the fair," Liz said. They'd been lined up on the table so customers could see choices. "Can you figure out when the set was stolen?"

A startled look passed over Jackson's face. "I bet I know. It's probably the one that was in the back of my car. I had some in the trailer for the fair, so I haven't touched that set for weeks."

A pulse of excitement ran through Liz. "Let's go check." At this point any information they could glean about the killer's movements would help.

Jackson smiled ruefully. "We can't. The police are going over my car as we speak. I have no idea when I'll get it back."

"For Horace's hair or fingerprints?" Sadie asked. "He never rode with you, I hope."

"Fortunately not. But I'm not sure the absence of evidence will matter. Just like the missing set. Who's to say I didn't dispose of the whole thing? And if it's still there with only that one leg gone, that looks even worse."

Liz had to admire Jackson's ability to reason under pressure. If it were her, she'd probably be sitting in a corner rocking back and forth.

"Good point, Jackson." Mary Ann put her stitching down and rose. "I'm feeling the need to lay this all out on paper." She went to a closet and pulled out a flip-chart easel used for classes. With Caitlyn's help, she got it set up, and—after fresh coffee all around—got to work.

With Liz's and Jackson's input, Mary Ann created a timeline of Horace's last night. Jackson had gone back to Crystal Lake and retrieved his card around eleven thirty. With so many days having passed, the police could only be sure that death had occurred after the last time Horace was seen, namely on the road when the couple was traveling home, at about ten thirty.

"Who did you see at the inn?" Mary Ann asked Jackson. "Let's not forget Horace went there that night and we're not sure why."

Jackson thought back, his gaze far away. "Everything was pretty quiet, both along the lakefront and at the inn. I didn't see anyone outside, and in the lobby, there was a young man working the desk. He had my card. The waitstaff had given it to him for safekeeping."

"So Alfred wasn't around?" Liz asked.

"No. I assumed he'd gone off duty," Jackson said. "Actually I didn't give his absence a second thought."

An unpleasant idea percolated into Liz's mind. *Had the innkeeper killed Horace?* "I think we need to talk to Alfred. I know he's an upstanding citizen and good businessman, so even saying that makes me feel terrible, but we need to explore every option."

"Think of it this way, Liz," Mary Ann said. "Maybe he can shed some light on Horace's last movements. He might even be able to provide an alibi for Jackson."

"I hope so." She realized something. "During that last trip, you didn't see Horace's truck or the other car on your way out or when heading back, did you?"

"No, like I said, the roads were deserted. I wonder . . ." He didn't need to complete the sentence. Was Horace already dead when Jackson had innocently driven past the fatal spot?

Liz thought of something else. "Jackson, if Horace died that night, then who vandalized your furniture?" Horace had been one of the main suspects since he held a grudge against his former boss.

"Good question. When I brought it up to the police, they implied I did it myself to throw suspicion elsewhere."

"Did you tell them about that strange call you got?" Liz asked. "The one demanding money?"

Light dawned on Jackson's face. "No, I didn't. And I actually got another one of those calls last night. I thought it was a prank."

"What did the second caller say?" Liz asked. "Do you remember?"

"He said, 'We know you have it, so give it up or else something worse will happen.' I thought it was some nutcase."

"That's harsh," Caitlyn said. "You'd have to be pretty devious to go that far."

"I suppose the police wouldn't understand why anyone would hassle me that way," Jackson said. "And frankly, I can't figure it out either."

"Unless there's some reason we don't know about," Liz said. "It has to be connected to Horace and his missing money."

Mary Ann tapped on the palm of her hand with the marker she held in the other. "The whole thing is strange, no doubt about it. All we can do is make a plan and start moving."

The group was quiet, pondering Mary Ann's words.

Naomi said, "Alfred and his wife gave a substantial donation to the apartment-house project. Liz, let's have lunch out there under the pretext of giving him an update. Which I do have, so we won't be lying."

"Go tomorrow," Opal said. "Doris will be at a women's auxiliary lunch at church."

"Can you get time off, Naomi?" Liz asked. "I thought Sweet Everything still had a booth at the fair."

"We do." Naomi pulled out a day planner and checked her schedule. "I'll have my employees cover for a few hours. The fair is winding down, so it should be slower anyway."

"I can come help if you need me," Caitlyn said. She gave her friend a cheeky smile. "As long as I can have samples."

"For you, any time," Naomi said. "Speaking of which, I have some double chocolate brownies to share if you're ready for a break." She pushed back her chair. "I thought a night like this called for chocolate."

"You got that right, girl," Sadie said as she followed Naomi to the snack table. "Between Horace's untimely death and the mysterious robberies at the fair, it seems we're in the middle of a crime wave."

Jackson turned to Liz. "That reminds me. I have the camera from my friend out in my rental car. You know, the small one he uses for game."

Liz was touched. "You remembered my pilfered vegetables in the face of all this? You're something else, Jackson Cross."

His cheeks reddened. "Well, if I can't solve my own mess, at least I can help you figure out a minor crime."

"What's this about a camera?" Sadie sat back down with a fresh cup of coffee and a brownie on a napkin.

Liz explained the plan to catch the vegetable thief. "The fence didn't stop the pilfering. We need to do something or poor Kiera's going to blow a gasket. She works so hard out there."

Along with the others, Sadie had been listening while she ate her brownie. After she swallowed the last bite, she wiped her mouth with the napkin and said, "Can I borrow it for a few hours? I think we should set up a sting operation at the fair." Her eyes gleamed. "We're going to catch that scoundrel red-handed."

15

"Where are you going looking so pretty?" Brenda asked Liz as she crossed the foyer late the next morning.

Liz, wearing a pale-blue linen skirt set, paused to talk to her guest. "I'm going to lunch at the Lakeside Inn with a friend."

Brenda clapped her hands together. "What a coincidence. Elaine and I were just reading about that place online. The food is highly recommended."

Liz checked her purse to make sure she had her keys. "It is good. I've had dinner there. Maybe you'll have time to check it out before you leave."

"I think we will." Brenda gave her a toothy grin. "Maybe today."

"You're not going out to the fair?" Liz was surprised by this news since as far as she knew the friends had attended the event every day.

"We're giving it a rest. All work and no play—you know the drill." Brenda headed for the stairs. "Have fun."

Liz spotted Naomi pulling into the drive and hurried outside.

Her friend rolled down the window as she walked toward the car. "Am I driving or do you want to?" Her dark hair was pulled up into an attractive topknot, and she wore flattering touches of makeup.

"I'll drive," Liz said. "Unless you have a burning desire to."

"Absolutely not." Naomi turned off her engine and opened her car door. "I'll spend the drive sightseeing. Or napping." As if to underscore her words, she yawned widely. "Sorry. That was rude."

Liz opened the passenger door of her car for Naomi. "You must be exhausted, running the store and a booth at the same time." Liz was tired too, and she was only a part-time helper at the fair.

Her friend slid in with a smile of thanks. "I am. The only thing keeping me going is the positive impact on my bank balance. And the thought that it's almost over."

Behind the wheel, Liz started the car and backed up. "Most of the vendors seem to be doing well. But, unfortunately, their new wealth is attracting a thief."

"I can't believe Mary Ann and Sadie were robbed. That is just terrible." Resting an arm on the open window, Naomi watched Pleasant Creek's streets and houses flash by. "I hope the new camera will catch whoever it is."

"Me too. The existing camera coverage in the place isn't adequate for the size of the crowds. Most of the time, the view they have of any particular booth is blocked by bodies. I saw that myself when we were up in the control room after Jackson's furniture was vandalized." Liz turned down a country road, one that was supposed to provide a shortcut to the lake, according to Sadie.

"The control room. It sounds so high tech." Naomi laughed. She pointed to a lovely white farmhouse and barns. "That's the Borkholder place, right? It's gorgeous."

"I think so too." Liz glanced at the rolling fields, noticing calves gamboling behind their mothers. "My cousin's daughters take care of those baby cows."

"There they are now," Naomi said. Indeed, two small feminine figures climbed over the gate and began to run across the field toward their charges. "Such simple joys. Seeing them helps me put things in perspective."

"I hear you." Reflecting on Naomi's words, Liz set aside her worries, fears, and plans for the moment. Instead, she feasted her eyes on the countryside, the shades of green adorning fields and woods, the deep-blue sky, and the black ribbon of road unspooling beneath her wheels.

"Did I tell you about the new bar cookies I'm testing?" At Liz's headshake, Naomi told her about her efforts to use local fruit, including raspberries, strawberries, and blueberries. "So far they're a hit. In the fall, I'll make them with apples."

"They sound great. People love all things local. I've noticed that with my breakfast menus. Fresh eggs and bacon are especially popular."

Reaching an intersection, Liz turned right as Sadie had instructed. Now she recognized the route she and Jackson had taken to the Lakeside Inn. If it had been safe to slow to a crawl she would have. She felt a little sick as she anticipated reaching the spot where Horace had gone into the water. Would this pleasant ride to beautiful Crystal Lake always be tainted with dreadful memories now?

"I'm sorry, Liz. I should have thought." Naomi reached out and patted Liz's hand, which clutched the wheel with white-knuckled fingers. "You went through a terrible experience out here. Do you want to turn around?"

Liz shook her head. "I'll be all right. My emotions are nothing compared to what Jackson is facing." She took several deep breaths, willing her tummy to settle down.

One last curve and they were there, at the scene. Several cars and trucks were parked along both sides, sightseers standing by the water. A news van was among them, and, spotting a man with a camera, Liz hit the gas involuntarily. They zoomed by, drawing curious and startled looks.

"Horace's connection to Texas big crime is all over the news," Naomi said. "Otherwise, the media interest might have died down by now."

"To be honest, I avoided reading the news today." Liz hadn't been able to stomach the speculation about Jackson. "Did they mention the money Horace stole?"

"I don't think so. Where did you hear that?"

Liz bit her tongue. Once again she was spilling the beans on Tommy. If Horace's stash wasn't common knowledge, then she wasn't going to be the one to broadcast it. All they needed was a countywide treasure hunt. Most likely whoever killed him took the money anyway. "Jackson said something about it, but maybe it's only a rumor."

"Probably. 'Man on the run with the mob's cash' sounds like the plot of a movie."

Naomi's attention was caught by the village as they slowed on the narrow lane fronting the lake. "Every time I come out here I wonder why I don't visit more often. It's charming." Today, families played on the sandy beach, and long lines stood near the hot dog and ice cream stands.

"There's the Lakeside Inn," Liz said, signaling to make the turn. "I have innkeeper's envy over this place." She eased into a spot. "But I've already decided the Olde Mansion Inn is just right for me."

Naomi laughed. "You remind me of myself when I visit big-city bakeries. When I get too jealous I have to remember that whoever owns those employs bakers and spends all their time coordinating staff. I prefer the hands-on work of a small business."

"And the residents of Pleasant Creek thank you." Liz switched off the engine. As she reached for the door handle, she spotted a familiar pair of heads bobbing up the path toward the front door. A groan escaped her lips.

"What is it?" Naomi, half out of the car, paused, studying Liz with concern. "Are you ill?"

"No, just slightly annoyed. Two of my guests are lunching here too." Liz shut the car door and pushed the lock button.

Naomi cocked her head. "This doesn't sound like you. What's the problem?"

Liz strode ahead to the paved walkway. "You'll see."

Inside the lobby, Alfred was presiding over the desk as Liz had hoped, but before they could approach him, two whirling dervishes in the forms of Elaine and Brenda descended on them.

"Liz! You made it."

"Who's your friend? What pretty hair you have."

"That's right, you're the baker. Remember, Elaine? We had her muffins at the fair."

Liz settled for giving Alfred a wave as Naomi, grasping the situation, quietly arranged to talk to him later. Then the foursome fluttered down the hallway to the restaurant, where the hostess settled them at a table by the window.

"Alfred. What a quaint name that is nowadays," Brenda said. "What's your business with him?"

They must have ears like bats. Liz fumbled for an explanation but Naomi fortunately stepped into the breach. "He's one of the biggest donors to our wonderful transitional living project." She sat back, waiting for them to take the bait.

"Transitional living project? Tell us about it." Elaine sounded genuinely interested.

Naomi gave the pitch as they waited to order. When the server came over, they all ended up with the same thing—curried chicken salad with grapes and walnuts on whole wheat and cups of tomato soup. The beverage of choice was iced tea all around. "We'll make a donation, won't we, Brenda?" "Of course. I hate to think of little children living in cars." Brenda took a sip of her iced tea. "We'll give it to you after lunch. I don't like to handle cash before I eat."

Elaine shivered. "Money is covered with microbes. But I prefer it to using credit or debit cards."

"The government can track you through your bank-card use,"

Brenda explained. She went on in this vein, citing news stories, until the platters of sandwiches and soup arrived. Then blessed silence reigned for a few minutes as everyone dug in.

Naomi nudged Liz under the table with her foot, a signal that she now understood the overwhelming nature of the friends' personalities.

"I wonder if bank-card use is making it harder for criminals to launder money," Elaine asked.

Liz almost sputtered out the spoonful of soup in her mouth. She hastily picked up her napkin and held it to her lips as she swallowed.

"Maybe you should ask him." Brenda pointed her spoon toward the doorway. Tommy Dunn stood at the entrance to the dining room, cowboy hat in hand, scanning the diners.

An involuntary groan escaped Liz's mouth once again, earning another grimace of concern from Naomi. "Another guest," Liz whispered behind her hand.

The friends missed Liz's reaction, as they were waving frantically at Tommy, practically bouncing with eagerness in their seats. Other diners turned to stare as Elaine jumped up and pulled another chair to their table. Tommy sauntered across the room, arms held at his sides as though confirming the existence of an invisible gun belt.

"What is he?" Naomi asked in awe. "A cowboy?"

"Something like that," Liz said. As one woman helped Tommy to his seat and the other flagged down the server, Brenda's comment floated back into Liz's mind. There was no reason to connect Tommy to a discussion of money laundering unless the friends knew his real identity.

"Hello, ladies." Tommy extended a huge hand to Naomi. "I don't believe we've met."

Naomi's cheeks flushed becomingly. "I'm Naomi Mason, Liz's friend."

"And the owner of a fabulous bakery," Elaine said.

"I'm Tommy Dunn, here from Texas." He flicked out his cloth napkin. "Staying at Liz's inn."

"Nice to meet you," Naomi said. Innocently she asked, "What brings you to Pleasant Creek?"

Tommy hemmed and hawed so long Brenda got there first. "He's a bounty hunter, hot on the trail of Horace Clegg. Isn't that exciting?"

The Texan looked mortified at having his business broadcast, but he didn't waste time on denials. "It's not very exciting when someone else gets to your target first." He crossed himself. "May he rest in peace."

"So the truth is out," Liz said. "How did that happen?" She was relieved it hadn't been herself who'd blown his cover.

"A reporter recognized him when he was coming out of the police station," Elaine said. She turned to Tommy. "Your website photo doesn't do you justice."

Tommy looked pained. "That isn't me—it's a stock photo. Think I want criminals to know what I look like? I like to sneak up on them, and then, wham! Out come the cuffs."

Brenda and Elaine giggled in delight. "If I was going to be arrested, I'd like you to do the honors," Brenda said. She nudged her friend. "Wouldn't you?"

Elaine's chin rose in indignation. "Quit that talk. We'd never do anything to get arrested for."

"I was just joking." Brenda fiddled with her half-eaten sandwich. "What brings you out here to Crystal Lake? Another case?"

Liz blessed Brenda for asking this burning question. Horace was dead, but his money was still missing. And she had the feeling Tommy wouldn't rest until he learned who had it.

Tommy focused on the sandwich the server placed in front of him. "Thank you. I'll take coffee if it's fresh and hot." He took a big bite and chewed slowly. Finally, realizing Brenda wasn't going to retract her question, he said. "I was, er, out by the site, and someone told me about this place. A man's gotta eat, so I came on over."

Maybe he was telling the truth, but Liz doubted it. How were she and Naomi going to talk to Alfred without big ears from Texas listening in and learning that they were investigating too?

"Alfred and Horace have the same last names," Elaine said. "Isn't that a funny coincidence?"

Tommy's ears reddened, but once again he feigned great interest in his food. Several french fries disappeared in one big chomp.

"Clegg's a common name around here," Liz said. "Right, Naomi?"

"There are Cleggs everywhere. Two or three in my high school class alone. Cousins."

"So they're not related even though Horace was living in Elmer Clegg's house?" Brenda's tone was casual, but the bright eyes fastened on Tommy resembled those of a hawk watching prey. "I heard Elmer was a cousin of Alfred's father."

Liz was startled. Opal had done some covert asking around about Clegg family connections that morning and discovered the very same thing. Where were these women getting their information? They were like ferrets.

Tommy's ears were like glowing beacons now. "I have no idea if they're related, nor do I care."

Liar, liar. Liz scraped the bottom of her soup bowl clean. "Naomi and I have an appointment, so I'm afraid we'll have to scoot."

Naomi set her napkin beside her plate and waved for the server. "Check for these two please." After the server trotted off, she leaned close to the table. "The desserts here are fabulous, but you have to try that ice cream stand on the beach. It's authentic frozen custard."

As hoped, the friends embraced her suggestion. "Yum, that sounds perfect. It's a lovely day to eat ice cream on the beach."

"Coming with us, Tommy?"

Of course the man was no match for the relentless busybodies, and Liz and Naomi were able to escape. Liz found herself striding through the dining room as if fleeing.

"That was something else," Naomi whispered. "Just wind them up and they're off."

"I know. But it was great having them question Tommy. That way we looked like disinterested parties."

Liz felt a pang of disappointment when she saw that Alfred wasn't behind the front desk. Praying he hadn't left the premises, she asked the young clerk, "Is Mr. Clegg around? My friend and I had an appointment to see him."

He gave them a friendly smile. "He went to his home office. Let me give him a buzz and see if he's available."

Liz and Naomi waited on pins and needles until the clerk finished his call. "He said to come on over. Go out the front door and take the side path past the tennis court. His house is behind that stand of trees. It's a big white bungalow. You can't miss it."

Following his directions, the women left the inn and set off through the grounds to find Alfred's house. Although intent on her errand, Liz was able to appreciate the flower beds, croquet lawn, fountain patio, and the court. The Cleggs certainly kept a luxurious and attractive inn.

"This is a huge property," Naomi said. "I didn't realize it had all these features."

"It's quite a spread," Liz agreed. In tandem with her appreciation, Liz was also tallying the labor and costs that went into the upkeep of such a large property. Once again she was grateful for the manageable size of her inn.

The gambrel-roofed bungalow was nestled among trees, with a private drive to the left leading down to the shore road. As they reached the edge of the house lawn, Liz spotted a dark-blue sedan. To her surprise, she recognized the bald OSHA official at the wheel. Had Horace turned Alfred in too?

16

Naomi took her arm and gently shook it. "What's the matter, Liz? You're staring at that car."

Liz tore her eyes away from the sedan, which had now pulled into the main road without stopping. Tires squealing, it roared off. "Those are the men who came to inspect Jackson's factory. The second time."

Naomi turned to stare at the road, although the car was long gone. "If it was them, what were they doing here?"

"Maybe OSHA is inspecting the inn too." Liz set off across the grass. "Let's go talk to Alfred."

An elderly housekeeper wearing an apron over a pantsuit answered the door. "Help you?" she asked with a frown.

Liz introduced them and explained that Alfred was expecting them.

Pursing her lips, the housekeeper regarded them dubiously. "Don't get him upset like those last visitors, all right? Doris will have my hide." She patted her chest. "He's on heart medicine, and he's not supposed to get excited."

Inwardly Liz groaned at this warning. They'd have to tiptoe around the topic. Forcing herself to smile, she said, "We won't upset him. Quite the contrary. We're here to thank him for supporting our charity."

"I'm not surprised. Mr. and Mrs. Clegg are two of the most generous people I know." She stood aside. "Come on in."

Alfred's office was in the rear, in a converted sunroom lined with windows. When they entered, he rose from behind his desk. "Naomi. How nice to see you." He nodded at Liz. "And you too." Although the man's face was pasty, his voice was steady. But when Liz grasped his hand to shake it, she winced. His hand was cold and clammy.

"Have a seat." He gestured toward two armchairs in front of his desk, then sank back into his chair.

"Before we give you an update on our project, I'd like to say how sorry I am about your cousin's death," Liz said.

Leaning back in his chair, Alfred fiddled with a pen, his gaze averted. "You mean Horace? Yes, that was a tragedy."

In another situation, Liz would have taken his body language cues and dropped the subject. But in this case, her friend's future was hanging in the balance. She couldn't afford to be sensitive.

"I understand he had only recently moved here. Were you close?" Naomi asked, an innocent expression of deep concern on her face.

"No . . . not really. We knew each other when we were growing up. But Horace was quite a bit younger."

"It's always sad when a childhood acquaintance goes wrong." Liz invested her tone with sympathy. "Or a relative. I know Jackson was disconcerted to learn about Horace's history."

Mentioning Jackson was a gamble, but it paid off. Alfred lurched upright in his chair. "I can't believe they arrested him. I've known Jackson for years. He doesn't have a violent bone in his body."

Liz went for the gold. "So who do you think did it?"

Again, the head went down and he began twiddling the pen, spinning it between his forefingers and thumbs. "I have no idea. All I can think is that Horace must have made an enemy."

Liz lowered her voice. "An enemy here? Or there?"

Alfred snapped the pen down, his lips pressed tightly together. "I have no idea," he said again.

"Forgive me for asking, but is OSHA investigating you? I thought I saw two government employees leaving as we arrived."

The innkeeper frowned. "I have no idea what you're talking about."

Liz didn't blame him for his denial. If word got out, that wouldn't be good for the inn, even if the investigators found nothing.

Alfred swiveled back and forth in his chair, playing with his papers. "I'm pretty busy, so can we move on? How's the apartment house coming?"

At Liz's nod, Naomi pulled out a report she'd put together. "This is how much money we've raised and what we've done to date." Standing, she moved to his side to show him the report.

"Hold on a minute. Let me get this mess out of the way." Alfred grabbed a stack of folders and papers and lifted them. Several slipped from his grasp and dropped to the floor, scattering everywhere. "Whoops. I'm all thumbs today." He gave a halfhearted chuckle.

"Let me help you," Naomi offered. She gathered the papers and folders, and handed them back to him. He dumped them on top of another pile on the desk.

"Thanks. Let me see what you've got." Squinting, he leaned forward to study Naomi's report.

He's really nervous about something. Liz noticed a bead of sweat trickling down Alfred's forehead as he listened to Naomi's explanation. As if sensing her eyes on him, he pulled out a handkerchief and mopped his brow.

"After the rest of the furniture is delivered, the first family will be moving in." Naomi moved back to her seat. "We'd like to invite you to the housewarming gathering. It will be small—a barbecue in the yard, so the family doesn't feel invaded."

"That sounds really good." Alfred glanced at a wall clock. "Thanks for the update, ladies. And now, I hate to be rude, but like I said, I've got a lot on my plate."

Liz rose. "We understand. Thanks for your time."

"And for your generous support," Naomi said. "We couldn't have done the project without you." Her smile was sincere as she shook Alfred's hand good-bye.

Outside the house, Liz said, "Alfred seemed awfully nervous, like he was afraid to talk to us."

"He sure did. At first I thought it was his heart condition acting up, but now I'm not sure. I mean, he dumped that whole pile of papers off his desk. That seems like nerves to me, or even fear."

"I wonder if Horace did the same thing to him as he did to Jackson—try to get him into trouble. If the prosecutor considers that sufficient motive for Jackson, then he'll have to look at Alfred too."

"Or maybe there's another reason. They were relatives, so there might be a history of animosity. Or maybe he just wanted to keep track of his cousin."

"Good point. We need to find out more," Liz said. "Dig into Alfred's background."

Naomi looked at her phone. "I have to head to the fair as soon as we get back. But I'll be happy to help later."

Liz pulled up in front of the Olde Mansion Inn. "Just focus on the fair and your business. That's important too. I'll spend some time researching this afternoon."

Naomi glanced at her phone. "Just got a text from Sadie. We're having another Material Girls meeting tonight. We're going to plan the big sting at the fair tomorrow."

"Tell the ladies I'll buy the pizza this time. Meet you all here at six?"

Naomi slid out of the car. "Sounds like a plan." She smiled at Liz. "Interesting lunch. Let's do it again sometime."

Interesting indeed. "See you later." Liz parked the car, waving as Naomi drove off.

Inside, the inn telephone was ringing. She ran to get it.

"Olde Mansion Inn, this is Liz," she gasped into the phone.

"Is J.D. there?" a woman's voice asked.

"I'm sorry, you have the wrong number. This is the Olde Mansion Inn." *As I said when I answered.*

"Isn't he a guest there?"

"I'm sorry, there isn't anyone by that name." *Unless . . .* "Is his first name John?"

"I'm not sure." Liz heard shuffling papers. "I'll call back," the woman said.

"Why don't I take your name and number, and if you have the right person, he'll call you back."

"Would you? Thanks." The woman gave her the information.

Liz decided to leave the note on John's door in case she wasn't around when he came back to the inn. As she climbed to the third floor, she heard voices.

"Want another snack, old boy? Here you go."

So John and his dog were here. She hadn't noticed the rental car. As she came up the stairs, her footsteps silent on the carpet, she noticed the door was open to the Sunset Room. She couldn't help but see inside—and what she saw was shocking.

John had laid out his purchases: candles, the quilt, and baskets. *All things from the vendors who were robbed.* Everything came together in her mind, in a terrible picture. The patently false name for the man—and his dog, who didn't respond to "Rover." The use of cash. The coyness about his purpose in town. The purchases at the burgled booths . . .

Liz stopped dead on the landing, frozen in place. *Is John the thief?* She needed to go and think about this. But before she could move, Rover came bolting out to her with a bark.

John followed, laughing. "Sorry about that. He does that if he doesn't hear someone coming." He took in what must be a shocked and appalled expression on her face. "What's wrong?"

"You're not who you said you are," Liz croaked, her mouth dry. "Your name isn't John Smith."

John stared at her a moment, then laughed. "You got me. You're absolutely right. My name is J.D. Jason Daniel." He reached down and fondled the dog's ears. "And this is Clancy. He didn't really care for the name Rover." He grimaced. "I don't blame you, old boy."

Liz backed up, sliding her hand along the bannister and reaching for the step with her foot. "Um, I've got to go. I think Sarah needs me."

His brows rose. "Sarah? I saw her leave an hour ago, just as I arrived."

"I have to call her, I meant." Liz turned to flee. She should call the police immediately, before he escaped.

His next words almost made her foot slip on the runner. "Please don't tell too many people I'm in town. I don't want the press to get wind of it. It will ruin my new television show and my producer will kill me."

Television show? Producer? "What are you talking about?"

"I'm J.D. Sykes, interior designer and soon to be host of a new reality show."

———— *////////////////////////////* ————

At a quarter to six, three boxes of pizza arrived. Liz carried them to Sew Welcome and placed them on a long table beside a pitcher of iced tea and bottles of soda and water. She tweaked a stack of napkins into place and moved the plates closer to the boxes. Everything was ready for their meeting.

Except a strategy. Although Liz understood Sadie's desire to catch the light-fingered crook, she didn't know how they could entice the person to rob Sew Welcome again. *The thief is probably long gone.*

The door to the quilt shop opened with a jingle of bells, announcing the arrival of Sadie and Mary Ann.

"Whew. We made it. What a day." Sadie carried her bag to the counter and slung it on top with a thump. "I'm pooped with worrying about Jackson, worrying about a thief, and running that booth." She turned to Liz. "How did you and Naomi make out?"

"I'm dying to know too," Mary Ann said, "but let's wait for the others."

Sadie grumbled but agreed. As she and Mary Ann unpacked their bags, Naomi, Caitlyn, and Opal arrived.

"Good evening, ladies," Liz said. "Help yourself to pizza, then Naomi and I will give you an update on our visit to the inn."

After serving themselves pizza and drinks, they sat in a circle, munching while Liz and Naomi described their trip to visit Alfred Clegg.

"He was definitely nervous," Naomi said. "Something is wrong there. I've never seen Alfred like that."

"I thought it was odd too," Liz said. "But maybe it had to do with those OSHA inspectors."

Sadie cocked a brow. "OSHA inspectors? Didn't they visit Jackson?"

"Yes, they must be making the circuit," Liz said. "Anyway, we're going to look into Alfred more deeply. We know Horace visited the inn on at least one occasion, and there might be something in their history, since they're cousins."

"I bet that Tommy Dunn could help," Caitlyn said. "I still can't believe there's a bounty hunter in town. It's like something out of a television show."

"Speaking of television shows, guess what I found out today?" Liz said. "My guest John Smith is traveling incognito. Don't tell anyone, but he's actually an interior designer named J.D. Sykes. His producer wanted him to scout undercover to find great pieces for a reality show. Then they'll come back and film."

The ladies exclaimed in surprise. "I've heard of him," Mary Ann said. "There was a write-up about a home he decorated in California. I can't believe I didn't recognize him. Or his dog."

"Yes, his dog is actually named Clancy, not Rover," Liz said. "And for a little while I suspected John—J.D.—might be our thief." She ticked off the reasons. "He used cash, his name was obviously fake, he knows a lot more about furniture than he claimed, and he bought from every booth that was robbed."

"Including Sew Welcome," Sadie said. "But maybe that makes sense in a twisted way. The best booths were targeted since they had the most sales." She preened. "I'm flattered J.D. chose us."

"He's a nice guy," Liz said. "He didn't even bat an eye when I blurted out I'd suspected him. He said he didn't blame me with how shady he's been acting. He's as angry as we are about the thefts and how they're hurting hardworking folks. Speaking of which, did anyone get robbed today?"

"Fortunately not," Mary Ann said. "I ran into Darlene on my way out and she told me that with the increased number of guards patrolling, the thief must have been scared off. No one was robbed today."

"To be honest," Liz said, "I was thinking the same thing. They're probably long gone back to wherever they came from."

"That's good news," Opal said. "It's over."

Sadie harrumphed. "I disagree. I think the thief took a day off so everyone would relax. Then tomorrow, the last day, they'll strike again."

"But isn't the last day of a fair usually the slowest?" Caitlyn asked. "Probably half the vendors are packing up already."

"Not in this case," Mary Ann said. "They've got a famous country singer coming. And a race car exhibit planned. Then after closing, there's a hog roast. I heard they ordered a dozen or more hogs to feed the crowd."

"That's a lot of pork," Liz said in admiration.

"And they're having a huge raffle. All the vendors donated something to it," Mary Ann said. "Tickets are selling like crazy."

"They sure are. Everyone who came to the bakery booth was talking about it," Naomi said.

"So it will be a good day for another robbery," Sadie said. She raised a fist. "Bring it on."

Liz sighed, reluctant to share her reservations and crush her friends' hope of justice. "But how are we going to lure them to Sew Welcome if they do return?"

Everyone was silent. Sadie's shoulders slumped. "I have to admit I can't figure out that part. They already robbed us, and they probably think we're too smart to get robbed again."

"Well, we are." Mary Ann's tone was tart. "I've been guarding our cash with my life." She patted her new money belt.

Opal, silent until now, gave a little grunt. Liz glanced over, concerned. "Are you all right, Opal?"

She waved Liz off. "I'm fine. But think about it. What do people use to buy raffle tickets that cost one or five dollars?" She paused and looked around at their blank faces. "Cash. That's where the robber is going to strike next."

"Opal, you are brilliant," Liz said. "Now we just have to convince the security team."

A rapping sound on the shop door drew their attention. Liz sighed. "Maybe it's one of my guests tracking me down. Excuse me for a minute."

To her surprise, John, a.k.a. J.D. Sykes, stood there, along with Clancy, formerly known as Rover. "Hi, Liz. I'd like to help you catch a thief."

17

For a moment, Liz was dumbfounded. Then she rallied. "Come on in, J.D. I'm sure everyone would like to meet you."

"Come, Clancy." Unlike previous occasions, the dog obeyed instantly, tags jingling and long ears swaying as he trotted after his master.

The ladies looked up with surprise when they saw Liz with her guest. "Everyone, this is J.D. Sykes and his dog Clancy." She went around and introduced everyone. "J.D. wants to help us with the sting operation."

Glances and murmurs of excitement were exchanged. "Your producer won't mind if your identity gets out?" Liz asked.

"No. I told him just now I've had enough of being anonymous. It was fun at first, but it got tiresome. I don't enjoy lying, especially to people I like as much as the people here." J.D. looked sheepish. "Fortunately, he decided it would be good publicity. That's how I got him to agree."

"So you're here looking for things for your show?" Sadie's eyes were wide. "And you like *our* quilts?"

J.D. glanced around, taking in the lovely wares on display. "I certainly do. I've decided to feature an Amish collection on the show and in the stores I buy for. Rustic simplicity and elegance—that's the tagline." He beamed, which was the most animation Liz had seen from him.

The women burst into chatter. Mary Ann fanned herself with one hand. "I can't believe it. This is incredible."

"I'll say." Sadie gave a whistle. "A wonderful ending to a tough week." She rose. "Please, have a seat." Everyone scooted over to make room for another chair, brought by Liz.

"I feel like I've made it to the inner circle," J.D. quipped. They all giggled in pleasure.

"Pizza? Iced tea or cola?" The ladies fluttered around the designer, making sure he had everything he needed.

"Are you looking for furniture too?" Liz couldn't resist asking. "I know someone who produces great Amish pieces. Classic and well-made."

J.D. stroked his chin. "I think I saw his work. Cross Furniture, was it? Too bad he's been arrested."

"He's innocent," Naomi burst out. "And we're going to prove it. Right, Liz?"

"That's right," Liz said. Her belly tightened with anxiety. They had to clear Jackson. Anything less than that was unacceptable.

J.D. had been following the interchange incredulously. "You two are investigating a murder case and catching a thief?"

"That's nothing," Sadie said. "Liz used to be an attorney, and she solves all kinds of cases."

"Very interesting." J.D. eyed Liz. "And here I thought you were only a wonderful innkeeper."

"She is that too," Mary Ann said. "So, Mr. Sykes, how do you think you can help us?" She clasped her hands in agitation. "I can't stand the thought that a low-down thief victimized us and is going to get away with it! And it's not just us—it's several other vendors too."

"What's your plan?" J.D. asked, one brow lifted. "How are we going to set the hook for the Bazaar Bandit, as they're calling him or her?"

"Opal, you go ahead and tell him," Sadie said. "Since it was your brainchild."

Opal sat up straight, looking J.D. right in the eye. "Would you be opposed to selling raffle tickets?"

———————— //////////////////////////// ————————

After everyone left, Liz retired to her quarters. The plans for the fair had been laid and, hopefully, would come to fruition. Now it was time to research Alfred Clegg.

Liz made herself a cup of decaf tea and settled at her desk, determined not to fall asleep. Using her laptop, she opened a browser and typed in Alfred's name and location. *Hmm.* Chamber of Commerce awards, Rotary member, hospitality magazine articles . . . At first glance, Alfred appeared to be an upstanding businessman and local resident.

But there had to be more. Liz typed in the innkeeper's name and Houston, Texas, just for the heck of it. A picture of Alfred at a convention came up. So he had gone there. If only she could find out if he visited Horace . . .

Someone rapped on her door. Closing her computer, she went to answer, knowing it had to be one of her guests since the inn was locked for the night.

Tommy Dunn stood there, a sheepish expression in his face. "Can I talk to you, Liz? I know it's late, but I'll only be a minute."

"No problem. Let's go sit in the library." An idea percolated in her mind. Maybe Tommy could help. "Want something to drink?"

"A glass of ice water would be much appreciated." Tommy followed Liz to the kitchen, where she filled a glass.

Liz handed him his water and led the way to the library, carrying her own tea. By mutual unspoken consent, they didn't speak until she closed the door and they sat.

"That was a fine piece of work you and your friend did today." Tommy whistled. "You shook me off like a cow brushing off flies."

"Sorry. We needed to do something and we didn't want company." She smiled. "Those guests of mine are pretty tenacious."

"Tell me about it. I had a devil of a time getting away from them." Tommy rattled the ice in his glass, studying the cubes as if they held answers. "So, Miss Liz, how are we going to clear your friend's name?"

Liz's heart skipped a beat. "You don't think Jackson did it?"

"Nope. Not with Horace's history." His eyes leveled on hers. "And with his cousin's situation. As they say, it ain't pretty."

"Are you talking about Alfred?" Liz held her breath, hoping the answer was yes.

"That's the one. I was hoping to talk to him today, but he skedaddled before I got there." Again his eyes met Liz's. "I kinda wondered if something spooked him."

"Maybe we did."

"Ah. I thought you might have been headed over to see him. Something told me a sharp lady like you would be on the trail."

"I don't know how sharp I am, but after seeing Horace at the inn the night he died, and finding out he and Alfred were related, well, I started to wonder." Liz sipped her tea. "Horace was killed practically under his nose."

"Did you find out anything?" At Liz's hesitation, he put up a hand. "I understand if you don't want to share. But let me assure you that I'm not just interested in finding the money. I think Jackson was framed, and if I learn anything that will help, I'll pass it along. And I hope you'll do the same for me."

Liz studied his face as she pondered his words. She saw and heard only sincerity. "All right, it's a deal. I don't care about finding Horace's money, but I do care about Jackson's freedom. That's my motivation."

"I respect that." Tommy sat back and waited, not pressing Liz any further.

"Let me tell you what happened." She took him through their visit to Alfred's house, how she'd seen the sedan holding the OSHA men pull away and noticed that Alfred was either nervous or ill. "Maybe he was upset about their visit."

"Could be. But I'll bet it goes deeper than that. It usually does, in my experience."

"Can you help me find out what it is? Let me go get my laptop and I'll show you something." She brought the laptop to him, opening the lid to display the photograph she found. "Alfred went to Houston on a business trip recently, but I don't know if that means anything."

"Let me get my laptop and do some digging. I have special programs on there."

Liz was elated. "Want some popcorn and cocoa? A snack to surf the Internet by?"

Tommy paused at the door. "We're doing more than surfing. It's called a deep dive. And yes, a snack would be great."

A big bowl of popcorn and two rounds of cocoa later, Tommy declared victory. "We got him!" He pushed back from the table, interlacing his hands and stretching. "It took a while, but it was worth it."

Liz hurried to his side. "What did you find?"

Tommy pointed to the screen. "I've managed to connect Alfred's visits to Houston—and Horace's gambling den—with big improvements on the inn property."

"So Horace was funding his cousin's business with gambling? Isn't that risky?"

"It sure is. About three months ago, it caught up with him. See the new loan against his property? Our friend Alfred had to go to the bank. But he wasn't doing anything new, just mortgaging the place. That means he needed money."

Liz pictured herself in those shoes, as a business owner. "I wonder what his wife thinks about it."

Tommy snorted. "If she's like most spouses, she's not too happy.

Unless he's keeping it from her. See this?" He showed her a deed. "It's all in his name only. So she wouldn't necessarily know."

"But if she found out . . ." Liz could imagine the sparks that would fly. "Do you think—"

Tommy was already there. "That Horace was blackmailing him? Probably. Not only would it be bad for his wife to find out, but think about Alfred's reputation if the news went public. Any whiff of trouble and his business would be sunk, as well as his home life. People don't like staying in a place that's going under. Or is perceived to be failing. They wonder why it's not doing well and decide they'd rather not find out for themselves."

Liz blew out the breath she'd been holding. "Where do we go from here?"

He pushed a button, sending pages to Liz's printer. "I'll see that the police get copies of all this. That's about all we can do right now, unless more evidence comes to light."

"I hope they don't brush it off," Liz said. "I get the feeling they think the case against Jackson is pretty solid."

Tommy tapped his fingers on the desk. "Me too. But really all they have is the table leg and Jackson being in the vicinity. Yes, Horace setting OSHA on him could be construed as motive, but it's not evidence. Alfred lives near where the car went in the water, as do dozens of other people. And anyone could have stolen that table leg."

"That's what I thought. Jackson said he carried them around in his car. We were parked at the inn that night—maybe it disappeared then."

"Good point." With another stretch, Tommy stood. "Well, I'm going to get some shut-eye. I suggest you do the same. I've learned the hard way you can't think about cases constantly or you lose your edge."

Easy to say when it's not your friend's life on the line. But Liz merely said, "Thanks for your help. I truly appreciate it." And she did.

Liz arrived early at the fair, eager to see if the planned sting operation would work. Maybe they would also recover the stolen money. Outside the front entrance, a booth had been set up to sell raffle tickets and promote other events to be held later that day. *Country Concert in the Main Grandstand*, and *Hog Roast Tonight*, read two of the signs. No wonder the tickets were selling like hotcakes.

In addition to fair staff, John—or rather J.D.—was behind the counter with Clancy. *Win a Home Makeover from J.D.*, read yet another sign. This ticket cost five dollars and was popular, judging by the number of people waiting to buy a ticket. Liz got in J.D.'s line.

"You live in a double-wide, ma'am?" J.D. was saying to the woman ahead of Liz. "Yes, I agree there can be decorating challenges in a small space. But that's where your personality can also shine."

"Is that so? Then please give me four tickets. The more I buy, the more chances I have to win, right?" The woman's laughter pealed.

"Hi, J.D., how are you?" Liz asked after the customer left.

J.D. grinned. "Great, thanks. Now, you're the one person at the fair who doesn't need decorating help. Your inn is perfect just the way it is."

Liz was flattered. "Can I quote you on that?"

"Sure, if you think my opinion matters."

She pointed to the line behind her. "These folks seem to think so." She handed him a five, watching closely as he opened a cashbox and deposited it, then gave her a ticket to fill out. "Is everything all set?"

He glanced meaningfully toward the corner of the booth. Looking in that direction, Liz noticed the camera borrowed from Jackson's friend nestled in the leaves of a bushy plant. "In a while I'm going to be taking a break, leaving my partner all alone." He thrust his chin toward the woman selling regular raffle tickets. "I think that's when we'll see a little action."

"See you then." Liz took her ticket stub and moved out of the line, the person behind her quickly pushing into the vacated space. The Sew Welcome ladies had sworn they didn't need help, so Liz headed for the food court. There she bought a coffee and a pumpkin muffin from Naomi.

"All systems are go?" Naomi asked as she poured Liz a coffee and bagged the muffin.

"They appear to be." Liz handed her several bills. "By the way, regarding the, er, other matter, I learned something interesting last night. Let's catch up later."

"Ooh. That sounds intriguing." Naomi gave a mock pout. "And you're going to torture me by making me wait."

"I don't have much choice," Liz said as the person behind her bumped her elbow. "Your fans are pretty demanding."

Naomi laughed. "They are that."

Liz found a seat at a two-top table in a corner. There she could enjoy her snack while watching the endless activity. She was daydreaming, pinching off bites of muffin, when a man wearing sunglasses slid into the other chair.

"Hey!" Startled, she glared at the intruder.

"Sorry if I scared you," he said with a grin. Jackson.

"What are you doing here? Weren't you . . .?" Her voice trailed off.

"Kicked out? Yes. But it's all right. I'm not here for Cross Furniture." Folding his arms across his chest, he grinned. "I'm here to help catch the Bazaar Bandit."

"Sadie recruited you." It wasn't a question.

"Yep. I'm prowling around the fair keeping my eyes open for suspicious activity."

"Speaking of which, let me fill you in." Liz relayed what she and Tommy had learned about Alfred's activities.

Jackson groaned. "I hate hearing that. What a shame. Alfred and Doris have built up a great business and done a lot for the community."

Liz's heart swelled with admiration for Jackson. Despite being wrongly accused, his reaction to hearing about another possible suspect was dismay, not glee. "I know. I wasn't thrilled to hear about Alfred's troubles either. But it's important for the truth to come out, no matter how ugly."

He sighed. "I know you're right. Horace wasn't easy, but he didn't deserve death."

"No one does." The reminder stole the rest of Liz's appetite.

The noise level in the food court, already high, ratcheted up a notch. People began to run from the area. "What's going on?" James asked a man vacating his seat.

"Didn't you hear? They just caught the Bazaar Bandit."

18

"They caught the bandit and I missed it?" Jackson jumped up from his seat. "Sadie will have my hide. Coming, Liz?"

"You better believe it." Liz traveled in the mayor's wake, thankful for the opening his broad shoulders created in the crowd.

In the front vestibule, Sadie spotted them and waved, pushing through the tight-packed bodies. "Liz, Jackson, we did it!"

Near the raffle ticket booth, J.D. and Clancy stood watching as Chief Houghton cuffed the thief—and Officer Jack Gerst cuffed the other.

Brenda and Elaine.

Liz gasped. "Those two? I can't believe it." Then she remembered there hadn't been any thefts the day before, when they had gone to Crystal Lake.

"They were working together," Sadie said. "One would distract the merchant while the other one cleaned out the cash. Ingenious, really."

"We'll send for our luggage," Brenda said as she trudged past Liz, guided by Officer Dixon. "At least we paid in advance."

Elaine followed, a little less willingly. She glared at the handsome young officer. "You're making a big mistake, you know."

Gerst's face was set like stone. "Come along, ma'am. It will go better if you cooperate."

Elaine's response was a peal of unpleasant laughter. "Like I haven't heard that before."

"Wow." Mary Ann joined Liz and the others. "I never would have guessed."

"That's how they got away with it," Jackson said. "To all appearances, they're two middle-aged gals just out to have fun."

Liz turned to the chief. "You really need to check out their rooms."

"We'll be right over with a team, Liz." The chief nodded at Sadie and Mary Ann. "Good work, you two, on setting this up. Hopefully we'll recover what you lost."

"It wasn't just us," Mary Ann said. "All the Material Girls helped. And J.D. Sykes and his dog too."

A young woman holding a reporter's pad pushed her way into the group. "J.D. Sykes was in on the sting?"

"That's my cue," Jackson whispered in Liz's ear. He melted away into the crowd.

"Why don't you ask him about that yourself?" Sadie said, turning the reporter in the right direction.

"I'm going to head back to the inn," Liz said. "Good work, ladies." She frowned. "Although I'm sorry I was harboring two criminals. I had no idea."

"How could you?" Sadie said with a harrumph. "You can't do a background check on every guest."

"Besides most of them are wonderful, aren't they?" Mary Ann smiled at J.D. Sykes, who was fielding press questions like the pro he was.

"They certainly are. See you later."

"Come back for the hog roast," Sadie called. "We'll buy you a ticket."

"Maybe I will. Can I let you know later, see how I feel?" Liz wasn't sure if she had the appetite for such an event. When she stepped outside and saw the roasters lined up with smoke pouring from them, she was even less certain.

An elderly man walking into the hall saw her expression and cackled. He jerked a thumb at the barbecues. "That's some of the best eating right there. The fire burns off all the fat but leaves the flavor."

"I'll take your word for it," she said. *Where did I park?* Liz studied the rows of vehicles stretching into the distance. *Ah, there I am.* Liz pointed herself in the right direction.

Several cruisers were parked outside the inn when she arrived. As she pulled in, Sarah burst through the front door. "The police are here and they have a search warrant."

Liz joined her on the porch. "It's all right, Sarah. Let them look. They'll want to see the Rose of Sharon Room and the Amish Room."

Sarah's brows knit in confusion. "Where Elaine and Brenda are staying? But why?"

"They're responsible for robbing vendors at the fair. They were caught red-handed today."

"Oh, that is terrible. They seemed like such sweet ladies too." Sarah led the way back inside.

Chief Houghton and his team were hovering in the foyer. Liz took the paperwork the chief handed her and scanned it. "Go ahead upstairs, Chief. Sarah will let you into the rooms."

They trooped upstairs and Liz fled to the kitchen to put on a pot of coffee. She was pouring a mug when Sarah came in.

"I'm shocked by this." The young woman looked close to tears. "How could we be so deceived?"

"Want coffee?" Liz poured Sarah a mug and joined her at the table. "I'm still trying to wrap my mind around it myself." She thought back. She couldn't think of any clues she could have spotted.

"Liz?" Chief Houghton stood in the kitchen door. "I think we've got everything we need. You're free to clean the rooms."

Liz stood. "Thanks, chief. Sarah and I were just saying how surprised we are about this turn of events. I never even suspected them."

"Don't feel bad, Liz. We just got some intel based on fingerprints. This is not their first theft, so they're probably expert scammers."

Liz exchanged glances with Sarah. "What do you mean?"

"Their real names are Betty Barnes and Stephanie Melrose. They're from Des Moines, not Sioux City. Previous exploits have earned them the nickname The Burgling Busybodies, since nosiness is their method of scoping out jobs. We thought they were in retirement after their last stint in jail, but apparently they decided to go back to work."

"I hope they're retired for good after this," Liz said. "They've caused so much grief and turmoil."

Sarah rose, smoothing her apron. "I'll go up and get started. The sooner we clean the rooms, the sooner we can put this behind us."

"Good thought, Sarah. I'll join you in a minute." Liz turned to the chief. "Do you have a minute for a cup of coffee?" He hesitated, so she added, "I have some information you'll want to hear."

"All right. Let me see my team off." When he returned a couple of minutes later, Liz ushered him to a chair and served him coffee and cookies.

"I figured you could use a snack after the day you've had," she said, refilling her own cup.

"Make that, after the week I've had." The chief's face sagged briefly and Liz noticed the bags under his eyes. It must have taken quite a toll to arrest a man he considered a friend. "What's this about?"

While the chief was gone, Liz had decided on her approach. In the past, the chief hadn't been that keen on her interfering with investigations. Nor did she want to imply that he wasn't doing his job since she genuinely liked and respected the man.

"I learned something very troubling yesterday." She told him about the discovery of Alfred's gambling and the new mortgage on the inn.

"That is a problem—for Alfred. But I need something to connect him to the crime." His eyes narrowed. "How'd you find out all that about Alfred?"

"Tommy Dunn helped me," she admitted.

"Dunn? I told him to keep his nose out." Houghton snorted. "He's just after the reward money."

"Maybe he is, but I asked him to help me. As a licensed investigator, he has access to databases I don't, since I don't practice law anymore."

Doubt flickered in the chief's eyes. Liz pressed her advantage. "Please, Chief, look into it. Jackson wasn't the only one out at the lake that night. He also wasn't the only person having trouble with Horace Clegg."

"I hear you, Liz. Unfortunately, like I said, we need more to bring to the DA." As she started to protest, he held up a hand. "But I'll probe the connection between Alfred and Horace a little deeper. That I can do."

"Thanks, Chief." Liz fervently hoped he would find enough to get Jackson off the hook.

Despite her reservations, that evening, Liz found herself seated at a picnic table with the Material Girls and Tommy, eating barbecue and listening to country music. "This is some good pig," Tommy said. He attacked his pile of pulled pork with gusto. "They even got the sauce right."

Liz took another bite of her meat. It melted in her mouth with its tangy sauce. She'd chosen coleslaw and baked beans as sides from the mind-boggling array of choices.

"Who wants to line dance?" Sadie asked, swaying her shoulders to the music. "My feet are itching to move."

Mary Ann stared at her friend in disbelief. "After being on your feet all day, you want to dance? Just an hour ago you were saying you couldn't wait to rest."

Sadie tossed down her napkin. "Well, I guess I'm rested. A little something to eat and my engine is stoked."

Tommy laughed. "Nothing I appreciate more than a lady who's dying to line dance." He gestured at his plate. "Give me a couple of minutes and I'll join you." He winked. "We'll show these folks how to cut a rug."

"You're on, cowboy." Sadie's cheeks pinked at the Texan's praise.

"Isn't that Wendy?" Caitlyn asked, nodding toward a woman in the crowd.

"Yes, it is." Naomi turned around in her seat and gave her a wave.

Earl and Austin were with Wendy and the trio changed course and came their way. The family was all smiles as they greeted the Material Girls and were introduced to Tommy.

"You can move in Monday," Naomi said. "We're going to do a few last-minute touches tomorrow, aren't we, ladies?" Her stern eye brooked no argument.

Wendy's smile grew even wider. "I just can't say enough about how wonderful everyone is in Pleasant Creek. I thank God that we found this place."

"I can't thank you all enough either," Earl said. "Once I have my surgery, I'll be able to work again and we'll be back on our feet."

"What kind of work do you do?" Tommy asked.

Earl stretched out big hands with long fingers. "Woodworking. But I got a torn rotator cuff that limits what I can do. Doc says surgery will cure it." He put one hand to his shoulder with a wince. "Once we're settled, I'll schedule it."

"Do you make furniture?" Liz asked.

"He makes amazing furniture!" Wendy's face glowed with pride. "You should see the fine work he does." Her face fell. "Unfortunately we couldn't afford to bring any with us. We had to sell just about everything."

"We still have my portfolio, honey," Earl said. "So if any of you hear about a job, please let me know."

"We certainly will," Opal said.

Austin, busy looking around while his parents talked, suddenly ducked back behind his father. Liz looked in that direction. Two men, one bald, the other tattooed all down his arms, pushed their way through the crowd, heads swiveling. Liz recognized the men from OSHA. *What was that all about?*

"Are you excited to have your own room, Austin?" Mary Ann asked the boy, who still hid behind his father.

"Come out and answer the lady," Earl said. "Mind your manners."

"Yes, ma'am. I'm really excited. Though the motel is nice too." His freckled face was painfully earnest.

"It sure is," Wendy said with a laugh. "Better than the Hotel Station Wagon." Her tinkling laughter was infectious and everyone joined in.

Warm admiration for the brave little family burned in Liz's chest. What a sign of character to be able to laugh about life's misfortunes.

Sadie leaped up. "So who wants to dance?" She smiled at Austin and jerked a thumb at Tommy. "I bet you can give this cowboy a run for his money, can't you, young man?"

Austin stared up at Tommy, a grin breaking across his face. "I sure can try." He turned to his mother. "Can I go dance?"

"Of course. Your dad and I will wait here for you."

Liz found herself pulled along and soon the Material Girls were tapping, sliding, and twirling with the best of them. Austin was adorable as he did his best to keep up with the much taller adults. But more than once, Liz saw the government agents in the crowd, their gaze fixed on their group. *What did they want?*

"Hand me a picture hanger?" Sadie asked as she climbed a stepladder clutching a hammer. "That painting will be perfect right here." The picture she referred to was a pleasant pastoral of farms nestled among rolling hills.

"Coming right up." Liz dug in the packet for the right size for the framed painting. All around them came the sounds of hammering, banging, laughter, and chatter as the Material Girls hung curtains and shades, stocked the kitchen with dishes and pans, and set out decorative touches.

Sadie deftly nailed the hanger in place. Liz handed her the painting and after Sadie hung it, she leaned back and studied its placement. "That look straight?"

Liz moved the left side up slightly. "Now it does."

Sadie hopped down the ladder and admired her work, hands on hips. "Nothing like art to bring a room together." Besides providing a focal point, the painting's colors complemented the decorating scheme in the room. An overstuffed couch and armchair sat ready to welcome the family, accented with end tables, lamps, and a coffee table of shiny maple. The overall effect was peaceful and inviting.

"I'm parched," Sadie said, flapping the neck of her T-shirt. "Want to take a break for an iced tea?"

"Sure." Liz fished a couple of bottles out of a cooler and they went out to the porch to sit on the wide front steps.

"Did I tell you we got all our money back?" Sadie said. "Well, we will once they release it. The friends confessed so there's no question it's ours."

"That's great news. I'm sure the other vendors are happy too." Liz was grateful that the matter had been resolved and her friends hadn't suffered financially. "I'm glad the women cooperated. Perhaps they'll get a lighter sentence." *Maybe they'll truly reform. Wouldn't that be wonderful?*

"They're on my prayer list," Sadie said. At Liz's surprised glance, she mumbled, "Pray for those who despitefully use you, right?"

"You're an amazing woman, Sadie Schwarzentruber."

Sadie pretended great interest in her iced tea. "Yeah, well. I listen once in a while at church." A shy smile played on her lips.

A throaty muffler from the street caught their attention. A battered station wagon pulled up to the curb and Liz recognized Wendy in the passenger seat.

"Our family is here to visit," Liz said, waving.

But the expressions on Earl and Wendy's faces were anything but happy. As Wendy rushed up the front path, she called out, "Is Austin here?"

Liz looked at Sadie, who shrugged. "We haven't seen him." The motel was a couple of blocks away. Had he tried to walk over?

Wendy let out a sob. Earl put his arms around his wife. His face was dead white as he hoarsely whispered, "Our boy is missing."

19

"Hold on, hold on," Sadie said. "Come inside and let's talk before you panic." She ushered the distraught parents into the house and settled them in the living room.

"This is our new place? It's beautiful." Tears poured down Wendy's cheeks.

"What's going on?" Mary Ann asked as the other Material Girls gathered around.

"Austin is missing," Liz said. "Earl, where did you last see him?"

Earl ran a hand over his mustache with a shaking hand. "He was playing outside the motel room. There's a little playground. We were keeping an eye on him, but suddenly he just wasn't there anymore."

The women exchanged worried looks. "Let's call the police." Sadie whipped out her phone and gave the information to the dispatcher. "The chief will be right over."

Naomi came and hunkered down beside Wendy. "We were going to have you move in tomorrow, but why don't you and Earl go get your things after you talk to the police? You can make this place cozy for when Austin comes back."

Wendy turned to her husband. "Do you want to do that? I'd like to."

He put his arm around her. "Whatever helps you, honey."

Opal took Naomi aside. "I'll call on some volunteers and put some food together for the family. I was going to do that anyway, we'll just move it up a day."

"Sounds good." Naomi bit her lip. "I pray that little munchkin turns up soon. I can't imagine what they're going through."

As the mother of an adopted son, Liz could well imagine. Steve had given her a scare or two, once going to a friend's house without telling her. She'd never forget the stomach-swooping terror of realizing she didn't know where he was. Her own prayer for Austin was deeply heartfelt.

The OSHA employees at the barbecue. A chill ran down Liz's spine. Austin had seemed to recognize them and had hidden from them behind his father. But from where? Questions bubbled to her lips for his parents, but she forced them down. Better to wait for Chief Houghton.

The chief was there within minutes, entering the house at practically a run. Officers Gerst and Hughes were with him. "What's this about a missing child?"

Sadie pointed him to Earl and Wendy, and he soon had the particulars down. Earl provided a recent picture from his wallet. "Go to the motel and question the residents," the chief told Gerst. "Find out if anyone saw something. Hughes, get a search team ready. We'll canvass the area."

"Yes, sir," Gerst said. He and Hughes left in a hurry.

"Chief, may I speak to you for a minute?" Liz asked. She didn't want to alarm Austin's parents if what she was sharing was a dead end.

"Sure thing, Liz." He accompanied her to the kitchen.

"I saw those OSHA agents—the ones who came for that follow-up at Cross Furniture—at the fairgrounds last night. Austin seemed to recognize them." She explained what she had seen and described the men.

Houghton frowned. "I can't see why he'd be scared of them." He gave a humorless laugh. "It's not like he's a business owner breaking the law."

"That's true. But what about the money Austin was carrying

around? The hundred-dollar bill?" After learning the boy was homeless, Liz thought his possessing such a large sum of money was even more problematic.

The chief gave a deep sigh. "I think we'd better ask Wendy and Earl about that."

Back in the living room, Houghton relayed how he'd seen Austin with the large bill at the fair. Liz confirmed that, saying he had wanted to buy a purse for his mother at the Sew Welcome booth and some sweets. "Do either of you have any idea where he got that kind of money?"

If possible, Wendy's face paled even further. "I have no idea. I swear I don't. If we had that kind of money, we'd have rented a place." Her gaze flew to Naomi. "We wouldn't take advantage of your generosity like that."

Earl patted her knee. "It's all right, honey. They're not accusing us of anything. Austin must have found it somewhere."

Pieces clicked together in Liz's mind. Horace Clegg's missing stash. The child's toy she'd found in the grass. The close proximity between the Clegg place and her inn.

"Did Austin ever play in an old barn?" The chief gave her a frown of puzzlement, but Liz ignored it. "I found a teddy bear on the grounds of the Clegg place the night the house burned down. Maybe it belonged to Austin."

"He did lose a bear," Wendy said. "Maybe it happened when Earl and Austin stopped by there. Earl asked the owner if he could do some handyman work. Austin was playing outside while they looked around the place."

Earl put a hand on his shoulder and rotated. "At the time, I thought I could do some light work. But then I tore the rotator cuff worse."

"Did Horace Henry hire you?" Houghton asked.

Earl's face reddened. "He was going to, but when I told him what

I wanted for a rate, he countered with less than minimum wage. When I tried to reason with him, he got angry and threw us off his property."

"He tried to take advantage of you," Liz said. *What a jerk.*

"You're lucky you didn't stay there," Houghton said bluntly. "Horace Clegg was involved in some pretty unsavory business. He did you a favor by not hiring you."

"I think the team should check the barn," Liz said. "Austin might have gone back. My cousin Miriam's daughters love to play in barns." She'd share her theory about Austin finding Horace's money later. The priority now was the child's safety.

Houghton radioed the station and passed along the order. But within minutes, the word came back. Austin wasn't there. Disappointment filled the room like a dark cloud.

"I admit that's a blow," Houghton said. "So we'll proceed with the search teams and canvassing the neighborhoods."

Later that afternoon, Liz returned to the inn to prepare a pot of spaghetti for the searchers. The effort was apparently going to extend into the night. So far, the only good news was the warm weather—if Austin was lost outside somewhere, at least he wouldn't freeze. Not that Liz thought he'd just wandered off this time, even though he'd done it before. No witnesses had come forward to say they'd seen him taken, but Liz couldn't shake an uneasy feeling. Her mind had made the connection between the mysterious money and the two men at the fair.

While the sauce simmered, she fed a hungry Beans his dinner. Enticed by the scent of food, Clancy came trotting into the kitchen. "I didn't even know you were here, boy," she said, bending to pet his silky ears. A moment later his owner appeared in the doorway.

"Hi, Liz," J.D. croaked. "We just got back. I was in meetings all day over in Fort Wayne."

"Are you all right?" In addition to his hoarse voice, Liz thought the man looked ill. His face was flushed and his eyes watery.

J.D. pulled out a tissue and blew his nose. "The short answer is no, I'm coming down with something. So my plan is to head to bed for some solid shut-eye before we leave tomorrow."

"Good idea. I can bring you up some chicken soup if you want. And tea."

His expression was grateful. "That would be so kind. Thank you. I hate to ask, but can you keep an eye on Clancy, make sure he goes out before bed?"

"Of course. He and Beans seem to enjoy hanging out together." Clancy was sitting near Beans, watching while Beans gobbled his dinner.

"I'll give you his food," J.D. said. "If you don't mind."

"Not at all." Liz made a shooing motion. "Go on up. I'll bring your tray in a few minutes and leave it in the hall. Put the dog food out and I'll bring it down."

Liz pulled a container of her cousin Miriam's chicken soup out of the fridge and prepared a bowl for J.D. Nothing could compare to Miriam's rich broth, perfectly seasoned chunks of meat, and fat egg noodles. Just smelling it made Liz feel comforted.

She put the covered bowl on a tray and added a pot of tea, a mug, and milk and sugar. Then she carried it up to the third floor and left it outside the door, grabbing the can of dog food and bag of kibble he'd placed there. She knocked twice to let him know his meal was there.

Clancy was eager to eat, so Liz fed him right away. Then the doggie duo curled up in the four-season room for a snooze. Liz finished putting together the pot of spaghetti and meatballs, along with garlic bread wrapped in foil. She put the food in a box and tucked in plates, napkins, and disposable utensils.

"How's it going?" Liz asked Sadie when she came to get the food. The task force had set up at city hall.

Worry lines etched Sadie's face. She shook her head. "No sign of him. They're extending the search area."

Liz's heart sank. The more time that went by, the less likely it was that Austin would be found. If he had been abducted, he might be miles away by now. "What can I do?"

"How about taking a shift manning the phones at city hall? That will give some of the others a break. Come down in an hour or so."

"I can do that. How about if I bake some cookies and bring them over?"

"Even better." Sadie picked up the box containing the food. "I'm sure everyone will appreciate them. And this meal. It smells delicious."

"It's the least I can do." Liz escorted her friend out and helped her load the box in the Jeep. As she walked back into the inn, she saw the first stars twinkling in the sunset sky. "Please, God," she breathed, "bring Austin home safely."

Inside the house, she checked on the dogs. They were still sprawled on the floor of the four-season room, snoring in tandem. A thought darted into her mind. *Don't basset hounds have amazing noses?* Quickly confirming that fact via a search on her phone, Liz dashed up the stairs to the Sunrise Room.

"J.D.? I'm sorry to bother you, but it's urgent," she called through the door.

The door opened a moment later and he peered blearily at her. "What's wrong, Liz?"

"May I borrow Clancy?" she said. "I think he can help find that little boy who's missing."

"Of course. I'll come with you."

Liz took one look at him, face flushed and swaying slightly on his feet, and shook her head. "You should go back to bed. I promise you can trust me with your dog."

J.D. nodded. "I know. Go find that boy."

Back downstairs, Liz went to find the teddy bear. She remembered bringing it back to the inn, but she couldn't remember where she'd left it. Hopefully it hadn't gotten tossed out. It required getting on her hands and knees, but she finally located it stuffed into a corner of the closet floor.

Holding it by the tag so as not to disturb what remained of Austin's scent, she went back to the four-season room. Hopefully her wild idea would pan out.

At first it seemed like a flop. Clancy regarded the bear with skepticism, giving it a sniff, then collapsing on the floor. *What now?* Liz remembered the garden. Austin had helped Kiera in the garden a couple days ago. Maybe there would be a trail to pick up from there. She hoped that if Clancy picked up his scent, he could lead her to Austin.

"Come on, boys. Let's go for a walk." The two dogs lurched to their feet, tails wagging. Beans showed rare enthusiasm for an outdoor adventure.

Not bothering to leash them, she led the way outside, across the grass to the vegetable patch. Liz held out the bear for Clancy to sniff, and then—praying he understood—said, "Track it."

To her surprise—and joy—he put his muzzle to the ground. Apparently picking up the boy's scent, he began to trot. Liz and Beans followed him toward the lake path, Beans finally wearing out and stopping about halfway to the path in the woods.

"Wait for us, Beans," Liz called. He gave a low woof and flopped to the ground.

Clancy stopped long enough for Liz to clip on his leash and then led her on down the path. He veered off on a couple of tangents, but he was leading her in one specific direction—toward the Clegg property. "I knew it," she whispered to the dog.

The police had already searched there, but maybe they had missed something. Maybe by some miracle they would find him. She'd heard of children hiding and being overlooked by searchers.

They emerged from the woods into the small field near the barn. The property was quiet, the ruins of the house still giving off an unpleasant charred odor, the blackened timbers lying in a heap. Clancy strained at the leash, pulling on Liz's arm.

"Wait a minute, Clancy," she said. She didn't see any signs of life, any indication that Austin was here. She thought about going home to start the batch of cookies she'd promised.

But having come this far, what would it hurt to check the barn? Obviously from the dog's reaction, Austin had been here recently. And the barn was a tempting playground for a small boy. Liz knew plenty of children in this area spent hours playing in barns.

She allowed Clancy to lead her through the heavy grass. There were two entrances, the big double doors facing the house and a small door at the rear. Perhaps animals had exited there to graze in the pasture.

The back door was ajar. It hadn't been that way last time. Her heart quickened, although she knew that perhaps a searcher had left it that way.

Clancy broke into a trot, whining and whimpering, as they neared the rear of the barn. "Hold on," she told him. "I need to open the door a little wider." Still holding the leash looped over her wrist, she pulled the door open. The dog nosed his way inside, pulling her through before she was quite ready. She stumbled on the uneven boards covered by loose hay. They were inside an old milking area.

The inside was dark, lit only by the gray light of evening outlining the cracks between wall boards. Trusting the dog's ability to navigate while her eyes adjusted, Liz allowed him to snuffle his way into the main barn. Here there were a couple more stalls, perhaps used for horses.

Clancy pushed unerringly to one in the far corner, his whining increasing in pitch.

Inside the stall, Austin sat on a bale of hay, his hands and feet bound and a gag over his mouth.

"Austin!" Liz cried, rushing to the boy's side. Clancy was there first, licking his face. "Come on, Clancy, let the boy breathe." She removed the gag. "Who did this to you? Are you hurt?"

He coughed, then said, "I'm okay. It was the bad guys."

"Baldy and Tattoo?" The nicknames slipped out before she could stop them, but she was rewarded by the glimmer of a smile.

"Yes. They took me from the playground at the motel and put me in a car. I didn't know where we were, but then they dragged me through your yard, by the garden, and brought me here on a path through the trees. They want to know where the money is. But I was too afraid to tell them."

Realization dawned. Those men were only impersonating OSHA agents, but they were really thugs on Horace's trail from Texas. She knelt on the floor to untie the rope binding his feet so he could walk. "We're going to get you out of here."

The rope was too thick and tightly knotted for her fingers to pull apart. Austin was too big for her to carry. She looked around. There should be something in this old barn that could help.

Using her phone as a light, she searched the stall and out in the main barn. *Aha.* An old thin blade from something. It was rusty, but hopefully, it would work. She knelt again and had just started on the rope when she heard the last sound she wanted to.

The big barn door slid open, squealing on the tracks.

20

Liz froze. Were the footsteps crossing the floor friend or foe? Judging by Austin's shrinking back and Clancy's warning bark, she guessed the latter. Thinking quickly, she slid the tool and her phone under a bale of hay.

Heart pounding, she turned to face the enemy. As she feared, Baldy and Tattoo stood there, sneering. Tattoo carried a camping lantern. "Oh, look. A friend came to visit," Baldy said. He stepped into the stall, the light making his shadow huge and grotesque.

Liz thought about grabbing the scythe hanging on the wall or the pitchfork lying nearby but she hesitated to introduce violence right away. "You really should let us go," she said. "Kidnapping is a capital crime." To her pride, she kept the trembling in her voice to a minimum.

"So is murder." Tattoo shrugged. "Six of one."

"Arson carries quite a sentence too," Baldy said to his companion. "I still don't know why you burned the house down. I thought you were gonna quit setting fires."

A sly grin slid over Tattoo's face. "What can I say? Habits are hard to break. Plus Horace deserved it for what he did."

Baldy shook his head. "He was already dead, bozo."

These men killed Horace. Are they going to kill us? She thought again about the tools. But one against two weren't good odds. If she were alone she might risk it, but she couldn't take the chance that they would hurt the boy.

Clancy growled from his corner and the men noticed him. "Get rid of that dog," Baldy ordered. Austin screamed and Liz watched in horror as Tattoo grabbed Clancy by the collar and dragged him out of the stall. "Get out of here." He kicked the dog's rump and sent him scurrying out of the barn.

Basset hounds weren't exactly guard dogs, Liz remembered. They were too friendly. At least he was safe now.

"What do you want?" Liz asked the men. Perhaps if they could give the thugs whatever it was, the men would leave them unharmed.

"We want the money." Baldy crossed the floor in two big strides, bending to peer into Austin's face. "The money this little brat stole."

Liz attempted a laugh. "Surely you're joking. How could an eight-year-old boy steal money? And whose money was it anyway?"

Baldy crossed his arms. "It belonged to my boss. And he's not very happy right now. First that idiot Clegg took it, and now this boy has it." Once again he leaned menacingly over Austin. "We found a hundred-dollar bill on him. Just one of many that were in the stash. We saw him flashing another one around at the fair."

"Maybe it burned in the house fire," Liz said.

Tattoo, who had been leaning against the stall wall watching, straightened. "Oh no it didn't. We tore that place apart top to bottom. Besides, Horace said it was in the barn."

"Shut up," Baldy snapped at his partner with a glare that could have peeled paint. "How many times do I have to say that?"

Panic twisted in Liz's belly. What was going to happen to them? "If we give you the money, will you let us go?"

Baldy's lip curled cruelly. "Maybe." Something jangled in his pocket. He pulled out his phone and scanned the screen with a grunt of satisfaction. "We're in luck. The old man is coming through." He tucked the phone away. "Let's head over before the coot changes his mind."

Were they talking about Alfred? Liz felt a flicker of hope. Maybe they could get a little more time to figure things out.

Tattoo's homely face broke into a grin. He rubbed his hands together. "About time. That slacker ought to know he has to pay up."

Baldy nodded toward Liz. "Let's tie her up and get out of here."

Her heart sank. She glanced at Austin. "Have you given him food and water? He must be dying of thirst." Picking up the cue, Austin began to cough.

Tattoo slouched toward the door. "That's right. I forgot to bring in his dinner."

Baldy crossed his arms across his beefy chest. "Hurry up. I want to get over there before the idiot changes his mind."

While the other man shambled out of the barn, Baldy studied Liz, his eyes raking over her. "Why'd you come over here anyway?" He smirked. "You could be sitting home knitting or something."

Liz debated what to say. If she told the men there was a huge search going on for Austin, would that help or hurt? They might take him with them, never to be seen again.

"I was taking a walk with the dog and he got loose and came in here. He must have smelled the animals that used to live here."

"How did you get in? The front door was locked."

"Back door was open," she said, trying to sound nonchalant.

Baldy continued to stare her down, but seemed to accept her story. "Maybe you'll have better luck getting this brat to talk." He gave her a leering grin. "Find out where that money is by the time we get back and you might be able to get back to that knitting after all."

"I'll try." Liz injected as much sincerity into her voice as she could. "I'm pretty good with kids."

Tattoo ran back into the stall, clutching a fast-food bag. He set it down beside Austin and pulled out a hamburger, fries, and a soda.

"He'll need his hands untied to eat that," Liz pointed out.

With a glance at Baldy, who nodded, Tattoo cut Austin free, leaving his ankles tied. Austin tore into the food. *Poor kid probably hasn't eaten in hours.*

Something rang under the bale. Her phone. Liz froze. Why oh why did that have to happen now? Couldn't whoever it was have waited five minutes?

"Take that." Baldy demanded.

Tattoo stuck his hand under the bale and grabbed the phone, holding it up with glee before he pocketed it. "We'll be taking this." Liz thanked her lucky stars he had found the phone instead of the blade.

"Leave them untied. If we lock the back door they can't go anywhere anyway," Baldy ordered as the thugs made their way out of the barn. Liz heard the sounds of padlocks being fastened and then the sound of a motor starting. They roared off, leaving Liz and Austin alone, thankfully with the lantern.

As soon as she was sure it was safe, Liz fished out the blade and began to saw at the rope binding Austin's ankles.

"Thanks for helping me, ma'am," he said politely. "I'm sorry to get you in trouble."

"It's not your fault, Austin. Baldy and Tattoo are the ones responsible." There. The rope parted and she unwound it from his legs.

Austin laughed when she said their nicknames. "Baldy and Tattoo? Are those their real names?"

"Probably not. But that's what I call them." Liz sat back on her ankles. "Tell me, Austin, do you know where the money is?"

Ducking his head, he gave a tiny, barely perceptible nod.

"You found it in here?" Liz guessed.

"Yes, ma'am. I know I shouldn't have taken it, but I thought it was a secret treasure. Here, come look." He jumped off the bale and stumbled, his legs apparently still asleep.

Liz caught him. "Wait a minute. Stamp your legs and feet until the pins and needles stop."

He did as she said and she released him. He led the way to the back stall, where he showed her a loose board. Underneath was a cavity in the dirt. "I found the money in here, in a paper bag. I thought a pirate left it."

Pretty good description of Horace Clegg. "Where is it now?"

"In my suitcase at the motel."

Which meant it was probably at the new apartment by now. No way was Liz going to send the men to the apartment, thereby endangering other people. That meant they had to escape the barn before the men came back. She frowned. Or they needed a way to stall the men long enough for them to escape when they returned. There were houses nearby, so they just needed to run to safety once outside.

Liz looked around. There had to be something she could use. "Come on, Austin. Let's get busy."

A pulley used to load hay into the loft was still in place, ropes dangling. Liz found canvas, heavy old plow wrenches, and more rope. "What are we doing?" Austin asked.

"We're building a dummy," Liz said. "Let's go up into the loft."

Working together, they assembled a dummy from the straw in the loft. Their dummy didn't have a head or limbs. It was a torso of hay with a core of metal wrapped in canvas made a heavy cylinder. Liz fastened a rope to it and gave it an experimental push. It swung out from the loft right toward the doors.

"It worked!" Austin jumped and clapped in glee.

Liz waited until the dummy stopped swinging before moving to the loft ladder. "I'll put that back in place, then let's set up some more obstacles down there. I'm thinking buckets and anything else that would hurt if you bump into it."

The barn was full of rusty and mysterious metal parts. They dragged parts of hay rakes, plows, milking stations, and tools to the floor, arranged so when the men were stumbling around, they'd trip and fall.

"I want you to hide over there," Liz told Austin. A little half wall near the door would keep him from view. "As soon as they're inside and I hit them, you run, okay?"

"What about you?" Austin's eyes widened in fear.

"I have to be up in the loft. But don't worry, I'll get out." *I hope.* "Run to the nearest house and don't look back." She hunkered down, taking his arm and looking into his little freckled face. "Promise me?"

"Yes, ma'am. I promise."

Austin got into place and Liz climbed the loft, taking the lantern with her. After she was situated, she extinguished the light. Having the men enter a pitch-dark barn would only benefit her. Justice would be swift—and she hoped unerring in its delivery.

All too soon, Liz heard car doors slamming outside. "Ready, Austin?" she called in a loud whisper.

"Yes, ma'am," came the reply.

The men fumbled at the double doors, cursing when they had trouble unlocking the padlock. The big door slid back and one of them stepped inside, followed by the other.

"Dark in here." That sounded like Tattoo.

"Maybe they're asleep." Baldy said. In the lead, he took another step.

With a prayer and held breath, Liz let go of the dummy. It flew through the air and hit Baldy square in the head. He gave a muffled cry and fell backward into Tattoo, who also staggered back. Tripping over one of Austin's strategically placed obstacles, Tattoo and Baldy fell into a tangled heap.

Amid the cries and grunts, Liz saw Austin slip out, his little legs flying. She hurried down the ladder and headed for the wall to skirt the men, who were still struggling to get up.

She was only a few feet away from the door now and could feel the fresh summer breeze on her face. Then, like in a nightmare, a hand snaked out and grabbed her ankle. Adrenaline surged, flooding her limbs and making her light-headed.

"Hold on," Baldy growled. "You ain't going anywhere."

Spots danced in front of Liz's eyes. So close and yet so far. Then she realized she *was* seeing lights. With a roar of engines, vehicles pulled into the yard, their headlights blazing. Doors slammed. And dogs barked.

"Neither are you," she gasped, sinking to the floor. As men filled the barn, she was only aware of one thing—Beans, who trotted over and slobbered on her face, joined by Clancy, who followed suit. She put one arm around each dog and held them close, savoring their warm comfort. She was dimly aware of Chief Houghton, barking orders as the men were arrested.

"Are you all right, Liz?"

She looked up to see Jackson, his face creased in concern. "I'm fine. Just weak with relief, that's all. How did you find us?"

He reached down with a hand, helping her to her feet. "When you didn't show up at headquarters as promised and didn't answer your phone, a couple of us went over to the inn. We found Beans outside, and Clancy was there with a dangling leash. He seemed determined to come here. So finally we figured it out."

"Just in time," Liz said. Jackson helped her up and together they walked out of the barn. In the headlights, Liz saw Austin being embraced by his parents near their station wagon. "I need to talk to Austin for a second."

Jackson and Liz joined the family. Austin threw himself at Liz. "This lady saved me," he told his parents. "She's my best friend." Wendy and Earl both gave Liz grateful hugs. She quickly filled them in on what had happened, then turned to their son. "You need to tell them about the secret treasure, Austin. It's time."

He nodded. "The money is in my suitcase. I wanted to buy you presents, but I think I'd better give it back."

Earl and Wendy exchanged confused looks. "You're talking about your plaid suitcase, son?" Earl asked. "The one that holds your toys?" At Austin's nod, Earl went around and opened the tailgate of the station wagon. He pulled out a little cloth suitcase and brought it over.

While they all watched, Earl unzipped the top and flipped it open. Inside, nestled next to small metal cars, a few books, and a stuffed animal or two, were stacks of bills.

Tommy Dunn, whose instinct for money appeared to be unerring, appeared at the fringe of their little group. He gave a whistle. "And there it is, ladies and gentlemen. Horace Clegg's stash."

———————— ///////////////////////// ————————

"Look what we picked," Kiera said. She and Austin came into the kitchen, Austin lugging the basket holding goods from the garden.

"I found the biggest tomato," Austin said proudly, setting the basket on the table. "After we weeded."

Liz peered into the basket, spotting lettuce, tomatoes, cucumbers, radishes, and a small green pepper, the first to be ready. "These look wonderful. We'll use them in the salad we're taking to the housewarming." Austin's parents were hosting a potluck cookout that afternoon.

"Now that we've trapped that raccoon, we have plenty," Kiera said. They'd used the infrared camera to film the wily creature as he wriggled under the fence and foraged for vegetables. Liz was also sure that he'd been the one who had raided her trash cans in the shed. Using a humane trap, they'd caught him and taken him out to the countryside.

"Come help me wash the vegetables," Kiera said to the boy. As Austin went to fetch the step stool that would bring him up to sink height, Kiera added to Liz, "He's doing a great job. I think he has a green thumb."

Austin threw her a grin over his shoulder. "I hope so. It's better than a black thumb."

Once the produce was washed and dried, Liz put together a large green salad, supplementing the garden's produce with things from the farmer's market. Kiera and Austin went back outside to continue their work. When Liz glanced out the window a few minutes later, she saw Kiera instructing him on how to deadhead flowers.

Sarah bustled into the kitchen. "All the rooms are ready for the next guests checking in," she said. She noticed Liz standing by the window. "What are you looking at?" After joining Liz, she gave a laugh. "I wonder if he wants to learn how to dust."

"We can ask, but I think we know the answer." Liz moved back to the table, where she diced some scallions for garnish.

"I made a cherry pie for the party," Sarah said. "Isaac will be stopping by later to pick me up for it."

"I'm glad you're coming," Liz said. "I think this party will really make Austin and his parents feel like part of the community." The Material Girls were attending, as were other members of Naomi's nonprofit. Jackson, too, planned to make an appearance, and Chief Houghton and his wife were coming by.

Clancy trotted into the kitchen, followed by Beans. Sarah had to jump aside to dodge them. She whisked her skirts away with a laugh. "Those two are so funny together."

They were indeed the best of friends. Liz was sure that when J.D. finally checked out after his extended vacation, Beans would miss the other dog.

As if he knew she was thinking of him and his dog, J.D. popped into the kitchen. "I've got some business to take care of this afternoon. All right if Clancy stays here with Beans?"

"Of course," Liz said. "I'll leave them in the four-season room when we go to the cookout."

"I'll come get him for that, and Beans too, if you want. Austin wants Clancy to come to the party." His smile lit up his face. "I still can't get over how my dog helped save you two and catch those crooks. Did you hear the police are giving him a Hometown Hero award?"

"He deserves it," Liz said. They had tried to give Liz an award too, but she had refused. She covered the salad with plastic wrap. "I'm going to head over there. See you soon."

A while later, when Liz arrived, the street in front of the apartment house was lined with cars. As she drove by, seeking a place to park, she saw people milling around the side yard. Smoke seeped from two grills, and children ran and played.

"Look at all the people at my house," Austin said from his seat in the back. He sounded both proud and excited.

Liz pulled into a space and turned off the engine. Kiera opened the passenger door and went around to help Austin out of the back. "I've got some folding chairs in the trunk," Liz said. "If you two could grab them, that would be great."

She opened the other side of the back and pulled out the salad and a small cooler full of cans of soft drinks and water. Liz headed for the food table, enjoying the sun on her face and the slight breeze. What a gorgeous day for a gathering. Her heart swelled with gratitude for many things, including a new home for a sweet little family and a warm circle of friends. The scent of grilling burgers drifted to her nose. *And a good meal to share.*

Liz placed her salad on a long table with the other offerings. So many desserts had been brought that a second table stood perpendicular to the first, mothers shooing children away until after they had eaten the main course.

"Liz, I'm so glad to see you." Wendy came up and gave her a hug. Her face was radiant with happiness. "I hope Austin behaved for you."

"He certainly did." Liz turned to see that Austin was running around with the other children. "Kiera's been teaching him how to garden."

"Next summer we'll have a garden here," Earl said. "Naomi said we can use part of the yard to grow vegetables." The family transition program had made the decision to allow families to stay in an apartment two or even three years, until they were financially stable enough to rent a place or buy their own homes.

"He'll love that." A tall figure crossing the street caught Liz's eye. "Here comes Jackson." She smiled, grateful her friend's name had been cleared. Once arrested, Baldy and Tattoo—whose real names were Ray Kane and Wayland McCabe—had admitted that when they first found him, Horace had claimed he'd given the money to Jackson. While searching Jackson's car for the cash, they'd found and stolen the table leg to frame the mayor and keep police attention off themselves. They'd also made the threatening calls and spray-painted his furniture in efforts to intimidate him into giving up the stash. Chief Houghton had issued a formal apology to Jackson, and everything was back to normal.

"We have some other good news," Wendy said. "But we'll wait

until Jackson gets over here." She waved at the mayor, and he changed course to join them.

"Hey, boss!" Earl called. "Thanks for coming."

"Wouldn't miss it." Jackson's grin was wide as he shook the other man's hand and nodded greetings at Liz and Wendy.

"Boss?" Liz glanced between the two men.

"That's right. Earl is going to work for me once he recovers from surgery," Jackson said. "His skills are perfect for my factory."

Earl's chest expanded with pride. "I can't wait to get back to work." He flexed his fingers. "I'm just itching to make furniture again."

Wendy leaned against her husband. "And while Austin's at school, I'm going to take on a few housecleaning clients. Thanks to your recommendation, Liz, I've already got two."

"I can't tell you how happy I am for you," Liz said. "This is fantastic news."

"And there's more," Jackson said. He pointed to the street.

J.D. Sykes was strolling their way, Clancy and Beans at his heels. Of course the dogs smelled the grilling meat and, as a unit, turned and trotted that way.

"Trust Beans to find the food," Liz said, rolling her eyes.

The two dogs planted themselves near the grills, identical expressions of hope on their furry faces. As the cooks flipped burgers and turned hot dogs, they watched intently for something to fall to the ground.

J.D. joined them, shaking his head at the pets' antics. "I guess we all love a cookout." He turned to Jackson. "Did you share the news yet?"

Jackson shook his head. "I was waiting for you."

"Hold on," Liz said. "I have a feeling the girls need to hear this." She turned and called to the other Material Girls to join them. They gathered around.

J.D.'s twinkling eyes went around the circle. "As you know, I'm head designer for a large West Coast chain of stores as well as being a reality show host. Our stores are going to start carrying Cross Furniture dining room and bedroom sets. They'll need to, after our first episode. People will go crazy for them. We've just inked a deal with Jackson for the first big order."

Everyone burst into cheers and clapping. "That's great news," Sadie said. "I'm so happy for you, Jackson."

"I'm happy that I can continue to employ local people and help support their families," Jackson said. He sighed deeply, shaking his head. "It's amazing how fast things can turn around. A few days ago . . ."

Liz knew what he was thinking. A few days ago he'd been a murder suspect and had lost a plum order, then had been publicly humiliated by being asked to leave the trade show. Now Jackson was back on top, where he deserved to be.

"Hamburgers and hot dogs are ready," one of the cooks called. "Come and get it."

The group surrounding Liz began to move toward the grills and tables, eager to eat. Liz and Jackson walked together. "Thanks for helping me, Liz," Jackson said. "I can't say enough about how you and the other ladies figured out who really killed Horace."

"What are friends for?" Liz took his arm. "I hope you'd do the same for me if the need arises."

"Of course." Jackson laughed. "Although I hope it never comes to that. How about having dinner at the Lakeside Inn again soon? Last I heard, Alfred Clegg is cooperating with the police, so we should have a nice, relaxing meal."

"It's a date," Liz said. *A nice, relaxing meal.* Then she laughed. If she'd learned one thing here in Pleasant Creek, it was that small-town living was anything but dull. The next adventures were probably just around the corner. But as long as she could face them with good friends like Jackson and the Material Girls, Liz knew she could handle whatever adventures came her way.

Learn more about Annie's fiction books at

AnniesFiction.com

- Access your e-books
- Discover exciting new series
- Read sample chapters
- Watch video book trailers
- Share your feedback

We've designed the Annie's Fiction website especially for you!

Plus, manage your account online!

- Check your account status
- Make payments online
- Update your address

ANNIE'S ATTIC MYSTERIES®   CREATIVE WOMAN MYSTERIES®   Annie's Quilted Mysteries™   Annie's Mysteries Unraveled™

AMISH INN MYSTERIES™   ANNIE'S SECRETS of the QUILT™   Chocolate Shoppe Mysteries™   SECRETS OF THE CASTLETON MANOR LIBRARY

Visit us at AnniesFiction.com